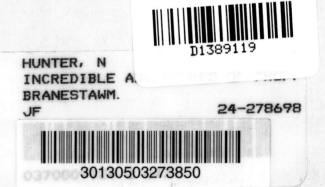

THE INCREDIBLE ADVENTURES
OF PROFESSOR BRANESTAWM

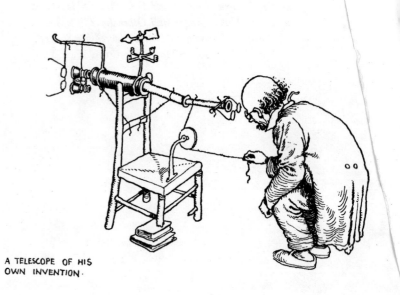

A TELESCOPE OF HIS
OWN INVENTION.

The
Incredible Adventures of
Professor Branestawm

NORMAN HUNTER

with illustrations by
W. HEATH ROBINSON

THE BODLEY HEAD
LONDON · SYDNEY · TORONTO

Dedicated to
Ajax of the B.B.C.
for whose inimitable manner
of reading these stories in the
Children's Hour I can never be
sufficiently grateful

ISBN 0 370 00992 4
Printed and bound in Great Britain for
The Bodley Head Ltd
9 Bow Street, London WC2E 7AL
by Redwood Burn Limited
Trowbridge & Esher
First published 1933
This edition 1965
Reprinted 1966, 1968, 1971, 1974

CONTENTS

CONTENTS

THE INCREDIBLE ADVENTURES
OF PROFESSOR BRANESTAWM

THE PROFESSOR'S
UMBRELLA.

—HE SIMPLY HADN'T
TIME TO THINK OF
ORDINARY THINGS

The Professor invents a Machine

PROFESSOR BRANESTAWM, like all great men, had simple tastes. He wore simple trousers with two simple legs. His coat was simply fastened with safety pins because the buttons had simply fallen off. His head was simply bald and it simply shone like anything whenever the light caught it.

It was a wonderful head was the Professor's. He had a high forehead to make room for all the pairs of glasses he wore. A pair for reading by. A pair for writing by. A pair for out of doors. A pair for looking at you over the top of and another pair to look for the others when he mislaid them, which was often. For although the Professor was so clever, or perhaps *because* he was so clever, he was very absent-minded. He was so busy thinking of wonderful things like new diseases or new moons that he simply hadn't time to think of ordinary things like old spectacles.

He had very few friends because people found it so very difficult to talk to him. It was like being at a lecture or in a schoolroom. Every second word he said you couldn't understand and he asked you questions worse than any you'd ever find on an Exam. paper.

But there was one man who was very fond of the Professor. And that was Colonel Dedshott, of the Catapult Cavaliers, a very brave gentleman who never missed a train, an enemy, or an opportunity of getting into danger.

'Well, well,' the Colonel was saying to himself in his usual brisk military manner, as he strode along the road towards the house where the Professor lived, 'it's quite a time since I saw Branestawm'—you can tell how friendly he was with the Professor to talk about him like that, not saying Mr Branestawm or Professor Branestawm or Branestawm Esquire or anything. 'I am glad he invited me.'

Yes, the Professor had invited him.

'Dear Dedshott,' ran the Professor's note, 'Come and see me tomorrow if you can. I have an invention that will change all our ideas of travel.'

You see the Professor could write quite simple, easy-to-understand letters when he liked. So the Colonel was going to have his ideas of travel changed.

He arrived at the Professor's house, when he got there, to the second. That was his military punctuality.

'The Professor's in his workshop, Sir,' said Mrs Flittersnoop, the housekeeper, who opened the door. 'He'll be out directly.'

The words were no sooner out of her mouth than a deafening explosion rent the air and the Professor came out of his workshop. He came out rather more like a cannon ball than a man welcoming a friend to his house, but he came out, which was the main thing. And most of the workshop came out with him.

When the smoke had cleared away the Professor put his hand to his head, pulled down the pair of glasses that he kept for looking at you over the top of, and looked at the Colonel over the top of them.

'Tut, tut,' he said, 'that was most unfortunate. I had a little too much of the whateveritis of the thingummy. I put plenty in to make sure there was enough. I'm afraid I've made rather a mess.'

'Not at all,' said the Colonel. It wasn't his workshop, so why should he mind? 'What do we do next?'

The Professor examined a piece of machinery that had landed on the geranium bed and pushed it into the back garden before replying.

'Happily nothing is damaged,' he said, 'so we can go on from where I left off. This is my new invention.' He patted the machine, which looked something like a cross between a typewriter, an egg timer, and a conjuring trick.

'Yes,' said the Colonel intelligently, wondering what it was all about.

'Listen,' went on the Professor, 'and I will explain.'

The Colonel sat down on the garden roller and started listening.

'If you travel by coach from this town to the next it takes two hours,' said the Professor. 'But if you go twice as fast it takes only one hour.'

'Of course,' said the Colonel.

'And if you go twice as fast as that it takes only half an hour.'

'Quite,' said the Colonel.

'And if you go fast enough it takes no time at all, so that you get there the moment you start. Very well'—the Professor was warming up to his subject and he leaned forward excitedly. 'If you go still faster you will get there in less than no time so that you arrive there before you left here. Do you understand?'

'Perfectly,' said the Colonel, not understanding anything.

'Well then,' went on the Professor, wagging a long thin finger, 'that means that the farther you go, the sooner you will get there, and if you go far enough you will arrive several years ago.'

'Come on,' said the Colonel, getting up with his head going round and round at the very thought of it, 'let's start. I'd like to go back to a party I was at three years ago.'

The Professor, eager to demonstrate his machine, took out a tooth pick, marmalade spoon and a pair of scissors, and soon had the machine wound up and adjusted ready to start.

'Wait a minute,' he cried and ran into the house, coming out a moment later with a small box.

'Bombs,' he explained simply, 'my own invention. Each one will kill an army. We'll take them in case of danger. Are you armed?'

The Colonel nodded and tapped his belt where he always carried his trusty catapult and a bag of bullets.

'Aye,' he said, and they got into the machine together, the Professor falling off on the other side and having to get on again, just as the Housekeeper came out with a cup of tea for each of them.

'Right away,' called the Professor, who knew all about railways, taking no notice of her.

The Colonel said nothing. He wasn't able to, because as the machine shot off the ground such a gust of wind caught him in the mouth that he could hardly breathe, let alone call out things.

Blue and yellow smoke shot out from every part of the machine. Wheels whizzed. Levers clicked. Little bits of stuff went buzzing up and down and round and round. And far beneath them the landscape rushed by quicker and quicker until at last they could see nothing but a grey haze all round them.

On went the machine, but nothing else happened. On and on they whirled, and nothing happened. And it kept on happening over and over again, till everything was so nothing that neither of them could notice anything.

Presently the Professor thought it was time to stop, so he rang his bell and put the brake on.

Gradually everything began to be something. The grey haze went and the landscape came back and soon they were descending into the middle of a large field.

'Are we there?' asked the Colonel, getting his breath back and using some of it at once.

'We must have passed it,' said the Professor, peering down. 'What's going on down there?'

'Why, it's a battle,' cried the Colonel, loosening his catapult in his belt. 'But it isn't a battle I remember fighting in. Anyway I can't see me there and I should be there if I was, shouldn't I?'

The Professor nodded his head, and then shook it to show that he understood.

'You weren't there,' he said, 'we're in Squiglatania, a foreign country. I know this battle. It happened two years ago. There was a revolution, but the King's troops beat the revolutionists. Those are the King's troops, the red ones.'

'Let's join in,' cried the Colonel, and at once he began firing off bullets from his catapult, while the Professor opened his box and rained his deadly bombs on the scene below, as the machine dropped slowly downwards.

'Gock, boom, smack pop boom. Twack boom clack plop

boom,' went the bombs and the catapult bullets, **and by**
the time the machine touched the ground there was hardly a
soldier or a revolutionist left.

'Hurray,' yelled the Colonel, jumping out and rushing
about, followed by the Professor.

'Hurray,' yelled a little band of revolutionists, who had
been hiding behind some rocks.   'We've won, thanks to you.'

AND SAT THEM
ON THE KING'S
THRONE. —

And before the Professor and the Colonel knew where they
were, the revolutionists carried them off to the Palace and
sat them on the King's throne, which happily was wide enough
for both of them, as the King had been a very fat man.

' Hail, our Presidents ! ' they shouted.

And bands played, fireworks went off, people danced and ate more than was good for them, to celebrate the victory.

' This is all wrong, you know,' said the Professor, ' it was the King's troops who won really. We've done something nasty to history, I'm afraid. I had no idea we should alter the battle like that.'

' Never mind,' said the Colonel, who rather fancied himself as a President. ' Let's do some ruling.'

But whether it was that the Professor, although he knew so much about everything, didn't know enough about ruling ; or whether it was that the Colonel, not being used to such high command, gave himself airs rather too much ; or whether it was that the Revolutionist people, who didn't like being governed by one King, found it wasn't any more fun being governed by two Presidents, things didn't go at all well.

First there was trouble about who should wear the crown. It was too small for the Professor's brainy head, and too big for the Colonel's bullet head.

Then the Colonel wanted to review the troops and there weren't any troops. They'd all been blown to bits with the Professor's bombs or catapulted with the Colonel's catapult, so he had to play with toy soldiers from the Palace Nursery. And of course no real live Colonel cares much about that sort of thing.

Then the Professor wanted to go on inventing things, and there wasn't an inventory at the Palace and nobody knew how to make one, so he had to put up with the chicken-house at the end of the grounds. But by the time he had got his wonderful machine inside it there wasn't any more room, either for the Professor or for the chickens.

' I'm tired of this life,' said the Colonel one day. ' Let's do something else.'

' What can we do ? ' said the Professor. ' If we get on the machine we shall only go back earlier and earlier and have to wait longer and longer.'

THE CHIEF
REVOLUTER

Just then the Chief Revoluter came in, sword in one hand and a bunch of keys in the other.

' We've decided not to have any Presidents,' he said. ' You're dethroned. Your services are no longer required, take a week's notice.'

' Don't take any notice,' whispered the Colonel, who didn't see why they should be spoken to like that.

'We refuse,' said the Professor, looking at the Chief Revoluter through all his pairs of glasses at once, and wondering why he looked so dim and hazy and funny shaped. 'Go away, there's something wrong with you. You must have

HAD TO PLAY WITH
TOY SOLDIERS ·

been sleeping with your eyes open, or else you washed your face the wrong way round. You're all out of shape. Go away at once, we're busy.' And he started adding up threes by the dozen on his shirt-cuff to look as if he had a lot to do.

' Stay,' cried the Chief Revoluter, waving his keys by mistake and quickly changing hands and waving his sword instead, ' get off the throne or be thrown off.'

' Ha, ha ! ' laughed the Colonel, who always saw a joke if it was an easy one.

' Ho, ho ! ' cried the Chief Revoluter, who was now very much annoyed.

' Hum, hum,' said the Professor, ' four three's are twelve, five three's are fifteen, six three's are . . . I do wish you'd go away and leave me to my accounts.'

' Guards ! ' cried the Chief Revoluter, banging his keys with his sword to make a jangling noise like an alarm.

' Yes ? ' asked the Guards coming in.

' To the Dungeons with them,' cried the Chief Revoluter.

' Gr-r-r-r-r,' growled the Guards, guessing that they were expected to be fierce. ' To the Dungeons,' and drawing their swords they rushed at the Colonel and the Professor, who got up and jumped out of the window.

' After them,' yelled the Chief Revoluter, standing aside to let the Guards chase them.

They dashed across the croquet lawn, where a lot of the Guards who didn't understand croquet caught their feet in the hoops and fell over, thus delaying the chase.

Through the grounds raced the Professor and the Colonel, down to the chicken-house where the machine was kept.

' We must get away,' panted the Professor, ' never mind where or when to.'

They clambered on the machine, and the Professor pulled some levers.

Zoom, crash, bang ! A terrific explosion rent the air. The chicken-house vanished. So did the Palace of Squiglatania. So did everything. And the next minute the Colonel and the Professor were rolling on the Professor's lawn, and the Professor's housekeeper was handing them a cup of tea each.

-WAS HANDING THEM A CUP OF TEA EACH ·

The day they first started had come round again and, of course, as they were on the Professor's lawn when they started, they had to be there again.

'One or two lumps?' asked the Housekeeper, meaning sugar.

'One on the back of my head and two on my knees,' answered the Professor, meaning bruises from his fall.

So they were all right again. The Colonel could go on commanding the Catapult Cavaliers, the Professor could go on inventing. But the people who write the history books had an awful time clearing up the tangle they'd made of Squiglatanian history by winning a battle for the side that really lost it.

THE WILD WASTE-PAPER

THE PROFESSOR'S HOME-MADE
SHOWER BATH .

The Wild Waste-Paper

IT was Mrs Flittersnoop, the Professor's housekeeper, who started it all, really. And once you started anything in Professor Branestawm's house you never knew where it would finish or even if it ever would. She was dusting the Professor's desk one evening while he was having some breakfast over night, so that he could get up early the next morning to do something important. And on the desk she noticed a little bottle marked ' Cough Mixture.' At least it was off the desk and in the waste-paper basket before she noticed it really.

' Dear, dear,' she said, ' how careless of him to leave things about. And no cork in it either. Well, well, that saves picking it up again, anyway.' And she dusted the rest of the dust off the inkstand and went to bed, leaving the bottle where it had fallen, with its contents leaking out all over the waste-paper in the basket.

* * *

The clock in Professor Branestawm's bedroom struck ten to seven the next morning, because it was one of the Professor's own inventions, and because that was the time.

' That sounds like Tuesday,' said the Professor, falling out of sleep and out of bed almost at the same time. In a moment he had whistled for a cup of tea. In another moment he had dressed himself with his usual scrupulous carelessness.

In five more moments he had put on his five pairs of spectacles, four pairs for different purposes, and the fifth pair for looking for the others with when he lost them.

'Now, let me see,' said the Professor, taking a sip of his morning tea and wishing it wasn't so hot. 'What did I get up early for today?' He pulled his near-sighted glasses down from his forehead and looked for the note he had made on his shirt-cuff the day before.

'Bother it!' he exclaimed. There was no note there. Tuesday was his clean shirt day. There was no time to be lost. Any moment now the laundry man might come and take his note away.

'Mrs Flittersnoop!' he called, and leaving the most of his tea untouched he ran downstairs about two at a time, but without stopping to count them.

He had no sooner reached the bottom than the study door was flung open with a crash, and Mrs Flittersnoop, the housekeeper, rushed out screaming. And well she might, for after her, flip flap, flop-a-crumple, came an awful mis-shapen white sort of thing with squiggly blue marks all over it. Just like a severely enlarged grocer's bill, which was what it actually was, only you're not supposed to know yet.

'Great gear boxes!' exclaimed the Professor, making a guess at what had happened and getting it right first time. 'Stop, hands up, get away, not today thank you, down sir,' said the Professor to the floppy thing as he ran after it. But it didn't seem to understand any of that sort of talk, so just as the three of them came tearing out into the garden he picked up a clothes-prop and hit it somewhere near the middle, whereupon it crumpled up all of a heap. The next minute a spare gust of wind caught it and whisked it away over the tree tops and out of sight.

' Oh, Professor, Professor,' wailed Mrs Flittersnoop, looping herself round his neck and going all pale round the eyes. ' I'm so frightened. Whatever was it ? Came at me like a wild thing, it did, as soon as I got inside the door. And me turned forty this twelvemonth. It's a shame, that's what it is.'

' No, it isn't,' said the Professor, who was thinking of something else. ' Pick up a stick and come back to the study.'

Back they went, the Professor very excited and his nose twitching like anything. Mrs Flittersnoop, very scared and nervous, but determined to go wherever the Professor went, for safety.

Then the Professor opened the door a crack, and they peeped in.

' Coo,' said Mrs Flittersnoop.

' Hum,' said the Professor.

The sight that met their eyes was enough to make anyone coo and hum, and make a lot of other astonished noises, too, for that matter.

The most unlikely things were going on inside the waste-paper basket. The pieces of waste-paper seemed to have had something that didn't agree with them, for they were swelling up and growing bigger every moment. One huge yellow-coloured monster like a gigantic sort of sponge was almost out of the basket. Others were slowly waving crumpled papery legs about in the air as if seeking for a foothold.

' Oh ! Oh ! What's happening ? Oh ! stop them, Sir,' cried Mrs Flittersnoop. But the Professor turned on her sharply.

' It's your own fault, you careless person,' he said severely. ' What did you upset in the waste-paper basket last night ? Now then . . .'

The overloaded, overcrowded waste-paper basket started creaking and groaning like anything.

' P-p-pup-pup-please, Professor, I never—that is, it wasn't, I mean I didn't, how could I ? . . .'

' Be quiet,' said the Professor. ' There are interesting developments about to take place.'

' Bang ! ' They took place. The waste-paper basket burst with a noise like a gun going off, and the swollen-up, monstrous, terrible-looking waste-paper came oozing and leaping out into the room in the most threatening manner imaginable.

' Most educational,' said the Professor, looking through all his pairs of glasses one after the other, while the Housekeeper fainted and came to again three times without stopping.

' Look out,' she screamed suddenly, pointing frantically into the room.

A huge piece of grown-up postcard, with its gigantic stamp glaring like an enormous fierce eye, had climbed up the curtains and was staring down at them. Then suddenly all the wild waste-paper seemed to rally, and it all came rushing at the door, bobbing over the carpet, the pieces rustling

—CAME THEIR PAPER

against each other with a noise like a thousand burst water-pipes.

'Run,' cried the Professor, and they ran. They ran like old boots, and like cats on hot bricks, and like everything that is rapid and frantic, and after them, bobbety rustle-ty crumple-ty whoosh, came the wild waste-paper. Huge, terrifying, gigantic, with paper arms waving and ink-smudged faces snarling.

'The pear tree,' gasped the Professor as they reached the vegetable garden. 'Quick, up, only safe place. Waste-paper can't climb trees—at least not pear trees—at least hope not—hurry!'

He picked Mrs Flittersnoop up with a sudden burst of strength that was quite unnatural to him and threw her into the branches, where fortunately her apron caught on some twigs, then casting a hurried glance backwards he scrambled up after her and soon they were perched on the topmost branches, swaying in the wind, and wishing nothing of the kind had happened. . . .

Out of the kitchen door came their paper pursuers, helter skelter, crumple rumple, over the lawn and piled themselves

PURSUERS, HELTER SKELTER

up at the foot of the tree still rattling and crackling, and seeming to be growing still bigger.

' Now, look where you've landed us,' said the Professor.

' Me ! ' she protested. ' Me, indeed—that I never.'

' Yes you ever,' said the Professor. ' Didn't you knock a bottle into the waste-paper basket last night ? '

' Yes, but that was cough mixture,' she said.

' Cough mixture my grandfather's second cousin,' growled the Professor. ' What do I want with cough mixture ? That was my special selected elixir of vitality, or life-giver, a marvellous liquid whose secret it has taken me more than a lifetime to discover. It brings to life anything it touches, and the only thing that will stop it is paregoric cough mixture. That's why I put it in a cough mixture bottle ; otherwise the bottle would be six times as big as the house by now.'

' But-b-b-b-,' began the Housekeeper.

' You see what it's done. Brought the waste-paper to life. Lucky for you the paper soaked it all up, or the whole houseful of furniture would be chasing us by now. Yes, yes,' he raised one hand, and in doing so nearly fell out of the tree. ' I know what you're going to say ; why didn't I put a cork in. Well, I didn't put a cork in because the elixir is ruined if you keep the air away from it. Nothing can live without air. Hullo, what's happening ? '

A movement among the pieces of paper had attracted his attention. Two of the smaller pieces had detached themselves from the crumpling mass and gone rolling and hopping back to the house.

' They're going back,' cried Mrs Flittersnoop excitedly. ' Perhaps the stuff is wearing off. Shoo ! ' she cried. But none of the other pieces went.

' Don't be silly,' said the Professor. ' That elixir won't wear off for thirty years or so. Wait, I'm going to drop lighted matches on them and set them on fire.'

He fumbled in his pockets, and then remembered he had left his matches on the bedroom candlestick.

' Tut tut,' he said, ' what a nuisance.' Then remembering that his memory wasn't very good, he fumbled a bit more and found he hadn't left them on the candlestick after all. They were in the lining of his waistcoat. He struck one, and leant as far out as he could, with the Housekeeper clinging frantically to his coat-tails to stop him falling. Then the match went out.

' Tut tut,' he said again. He struck another match and dropped it at once. But the match hadn't lit, so that was no good.

' Tut tut as before,' he said, and struck another. And this time he dropped it well alight. Down and down dropped the little flaming stick like a miniature beacon of hope, or an imitation sky rocket coming down, or even like a lighted match being dropped out of a pear tree.

' Ah-h-h,' went the Professor and the Housekeeper both together, but neither of them in time.

Then ' Oh-h-h,' they went, for just as the match was about to drop into the midst of the puffed-up awful wild waste-paper, what must it do but go and catch on a branch and stay there till it flickered and died out.

The Professor was just going to strike another match when Mrs Flittersnoop pulled him back by his coat-tails.

' Look, they're coming back,' she gasped.

And so they were. The two pieces of wild waste-paper that had gone into the house were hurrying out again. And

RUSHED AT THE
PROFESSOR —

they were carrying something that glinted and shone in the sunlight.

'Exceptional,' said the Professor. 'They're bringing a saw from the tool-shed. Surely they can't know what a saw is. Now, can it have anything to do with what's written on the paper? Would the elixir make a butcher's bill know a saw if it saw it, and if so does that mean that the gas bill which I threw away yesterday, and which I see below us, may explode at any moment?'

The Professor stopped thinking to scratch his head, then he went on thinking again. But he didn't have time to think much because all at once the tree began to shake and shiver, and above the crumpling rustling noise of the mad paper came the hoarse rasp of the saw. The paper monstrosities were starting to cut the tree down.

'Help!' shrieked Mrs Flittersnoop when she realised what was happening. 'Oh, do something—do something, Professor!' she moaned, shaking like a jelly and going all different colours.

But the Professor hadn't been listening to what she had said. He was busy studying the scene below through his long-sighted glasses, and making notes in several different languages on an ample pear he had picked.

The tree shook more and more as the sharp saw bit deeper and deeper into the trunk. Mrs Flittersnoop gave up talking to the Professor, and got more and more frightened. She began to think the silliest things, such as 'if you fall out of a pear tree is it a pear drop?'

'Amazing intelligence,' said the Professor. 'They've done it.'

They had. The tree gave a convulsive shiver and down it crashed, falling with such violence that the Professor and his housekeeper were flung over the fence into the next garden.

'Hullo!' said the next-door man, coming out of his potting shed with a dahlia seed in his hand.

He hadn't time to say any more, for over the fence, for all the world like a lot of huge crazy sponges, came the wild waste-paper. They rushed at the Professor and the Housekeeper and the next-door man, and there was such a scrimmage and a dust up, and a goodness knows what, as nobody has ever seen since.

Bravely the Professor grappled with the first piece, and

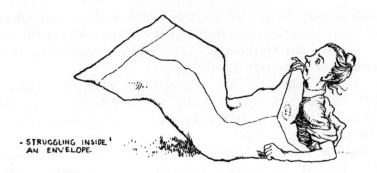

- STRUGGLING INSIDE
AN ENVELOPE.

tore it to shreds. But each shred swelled up and became a
separate monstrous thing. The Housekeeper was struggling
inside an envelope. The next-door man was all wrapped up
in a circular about corn cure, though he'd never had corns in
his life.

And in another second there would have been no more
Professor or Housekeeper or next-door man. And the wild
waste-paper would have had the upper hand, and everything would have been awful. But just at that very exact
moment the piece of gas bill the Professor was fighting stepped
on the edge of a bonfire the next-door man had been having.

'Poof!' went the flames, and the gas bill flashed up and disappeared in a handful of ash, setting fire to the corn cure
circular as it did so. Then the envelope with the Housekeeper
in caught fire and soon the whole crumply crowd of frightful
paper monsters was blazing and crackling away like a furnace.

'Oh, my eyebrows,' cried the Housekeeper. 'They're
gone—singed off.'

'And, oh, my dahlia seed,' wailed the next-door man.
'It's fried, baked, and toasted, so it is. I'll never grow any
dahlias from that now.'

The Professor mopped his forehead with the Housekeeper's apron.

'Thank goodness for your bonfire,' he gasped. 'If it hadn't been for that . . .' He stopped, leaving the others to fill in the missing words.

WRAPPED UP IN A CIRCULAR
ABOUT CORN CURE

THE PROFESSOR
BORROWS A BOOK

THE PROFESSOR'S
TROUSER ELEVATOR

3

The Professor borrows a Book

THINGS were busy in the library at **GREAT PAGWELL** when Professor Branestawm walked in. Some of the library men were feeding the book worms, others were rubbing out the pencil marks that people aren't supposed to make on books but often do. Others were looking to see if anyone had left anything useful in the books, which they never do, only old bus tickets and things.

'Good morning,' said the Chief Library man, who knew the Professor quite well.

'Good morning,' said the Professor. 'Two penny stamps, please,' then he remembered it wasn't the post office, and put down an extra penny, 'er—that is I mean a cup of tea and a bun,' he said. Then he remembered it wasn't a tea-shop either, and took his hat off to scratch his head and try to think where he was.

And when he took off his hat, out fell a great crowd of papers. They shot all over the floor. They fluttered under tables and out of windows.

OUT FELL A CROWD OF PAPERS

' Allow me,' said the Library man, and, jumping over the counter quite easily because he was very sporting and could jump gates, he helped the Professor to pick up the papers. The Professor picked up two and dropped one of them again, while the Chief Library man picked up the rest.

' Now, let me see,' said the Professor, turning over the papers and dropping some again, ' what did I want? It was a book about something.' He dropped some more papers, looked at the others through his near-sighted glasses, and then remembered he had written what he was looking for on the back of his collar, the night before. So he had to get the Library man to read it out for him.

' The Life and Likings of a Lobster,' he read out.

' Yes,' said the Professor, fastening up the safety pins which he had on his coat instead of the buttons that had all come off. ' One of those, please, not too new.'

The Chief Library man called a not-so-chief Library man, who called a quite ordinary, unimportant sort of Library man. And he went off and climbed ladders and got himself all dusty, poking about on shelves. And at last, when they thought he must have found an interesting adventure book and stopped to read it, back he came.

'The Life and Likings of——' he began, but the Professor grabbed the book out of his hand, opened it, and rushed out, reading it, putting his foot in the pail of soapy water the char-woman was cleaning the steps with, and getting half-way home with the pail stuck on his foot before it fell off.

The next morning the Professor could not find the book anywhere. He looked through his near-sighted glasses and his long-sighted glasses, and all his other glasses. He even looked through the glasses he used to look for the other pairs of glasses with when he lost them. But still he couldn't find it.

'Mrs Flittersnoop,' he called to his housekeeper, 'have you seen a book with one of those green library covers? It's about lobsters. I had it last night, and now it's gone.'

'No, Sir, that I haven't,' she said, 'and not that I'd touch it if I had, being most particular to leave things alone since I upset that stuff in the waste basket and made the waste-paper come to life.'

'Of course,' said the Professor hurriedly, so that Mrs Flittersnoop shouldn't go on and tell him about her cousin's husband's little girl, who was either just going to have measles, or had just had them.

Then he put on his hat and went across to the library at LITTLE PAGWELL.

'Have you got a book called "The Life and Likings of a Lobster"?' he asked the Chief Library man.

'Certainly,' said the man, and he actually went and fetched it himself.

'Ta,' said the Professor, and went out leaving it on the counter, and had to come back for it.

After a fortnight had gone by it was time to take back to the library at GREAT PAGWELL the book he had borrowed from there. But he had lost it, so he couldn't take it back.

'I'll have to take this one back,' said the Professor. So back he took it, and that was all right, because he was able to take it out again the next day and return it to the Library at LITTLE PAGWELL, so he didn't have any fines to pay at either place for keeping it too long.

Then he took the book out of the LITTLE PAGWELL library again the next day, and went home to read it a bit more.

'As long as I keep taking it back to GREAT PAGWELL when the time's up,' he said, 'and getting it back next day and taking it over to LITTLE PAGWELL, it will be all right, and nobody will know I've lost the other book.'

You see both books had the usual green library covers, so they both looked alike.

Then, what must the Professor go and do but lose the other book, the one that belonged to LITTLE PAGWELL.

'Dear, dear ; that *is* a nuisance,' he said, and he hunted for it like anything. He looked under the sofa, but all he found there was a bone Mrs Flittersnoop's sister's dog had left there weeks ago. He looked in the coal cellar and under the sink and at the back of the gas stove. He looked in all the places where a book isn't likely to be as well as all the places where it might be. And still he couldn't find it.

'Well,' he said, pushing all his five pairs of spectacles up a bit higher, 'I'll have to go to still another library and get another copy of the book.'

So he went and got one from the library at UPPER PAG-
WELL, took it to the library at GREAT PAGWELL where
it was just due, and handed it in. Next day he took it out
again, and gave it in at the LITTLE PAGWELL Library.
And so by taking it round in turn to all three libraries he still
managed to stop any of them from knowing he had lost the
books.

Then, bothered if he didn't lose *that* book, too !

'This is awful,' groaned the Professor. 'Whatever can
be happening to all these books ? It can't be the mice,
because we haven't any, and Mrs Flittersnoop does not read
anything but story books with paper covers. She doesn't even
read cookery books. I wish she did.'

He took off all his five pairs of spectacles, cleaned them
and put them on again, getting them all mixed up and
wondering why his smoked sun-glasses didn't magnify
things.

Well, of course, in the end he just had to go off to the
library at LOWER PAGWELL and get another copy of the
Life and Likings of a Lobster there. And he had to keep
going round with that one book to all four libraries, giving it
in one day and taking it out the next.

Then he lost that book, too. Yes, he did, the careless man.
And he kept on getting more and more copies of the book
from more and more libraries, and losing them one after the
other.

He had a book out of the library at PAGWELL TOWN
and PAGWELL VILLAGE. He had one from OLD PAG-
WELL and NEW PAGWELL, from NORTH PAGWELL
and from SOUTH PAGWELL, and another from WEST PAG-
WELL, as well as PAGWELL CENTRAL. He had one from

PAGWELL HILL and PAGWELL DOCKS, not to mention PAGWELL GARDENS.

Yes, he took copies of the same book out of all these different libraries, and kept losing them until at last he had fourteen libraries to keep going, on only one book.

Now each library let him keep their book for fourteen days, so the Professor was just able to avoid paying a fine for keeping it too long. But every day he had to rush round to the library that had the book, take it out, dash off to the library where it was due next, and give it in again. It was terrible. He had no time to read the book. He had hardly time for meals. He got thinner and thinner through having to dash about so much. And he simply dared not stop rushing from library to library, because if he once let the book be a day late at one library, the fines would start getting bigger and bigger.

' Oh, what shall I do—what shall I do ? ' he cried, trying to tear his hair, only there wasn't enough of it.

Then he went to see his friend, Colonel Dedshott, of the Catapult Cavaliers, to see if he could help.

' Lobsters ! ' said the Colonel when the Professor told him the title of the book. ' I like 'em, but they give me dreams.'

' Never mind that,' said the Professor. ' Tell me what I can do about the books I've lost. This rushing about is too much for a man of my age, whatever my age is. I can never remember.'

' Sorry, Professor,' said the Colonel, ' but I'm not going to get mixed up in any more of your adventures. All I can do is to lend you my bicycle to help you get round the libraries quicker.'

' Oh, anything,' said the Professor, and taking the Colonel's bicycle, one of the old penny-farthing affairs, with one very

—AND WENT WHIZZING STRAIGHT INSIDE,—

big wheel and one very little one, he climbed into the saddle and wobbled off up the road.

The Professor wasn't much good at riding bicycles, and he ran into three carts, seven lamp-posts, a pond, and several policemen before he got to the library at NORTH PAG-WELL, which was next on the list.

And when he did get to the library he couldn't stop, and went whizzing straight inside, scattering all sorts of studious-looking people about all over the floor.

' I beg all your pardons, I'm sure,' he gasped politely. Then, taking the book from the library man, he wheeled the bicycle outside, climbed up a lamp-post to get into the saddle, and rode off, leaving the book on the path, and had to come back all the way from WEST PAGWELL to fetch it.

Things went on like this for days and days. The Professor was getting quite expert at riding a bicycle, and could even read bits out of the book as he went along if there was nothing in the way. And the Library men got to know him quite well.

' What's going to be the end of all this, I don't know,' groaned the Professor, dropping wearily into his chair after a strenuous ride up from PAGWELL DOCKS. ' One book can't last fourteen libraries for ever. Something's got to happen soon.'

It happened the very next day. All the fourteen Library men came to tea with the Professor just after he'd got back from PAGWELL TOWN.

' Oh, how d'ye do,' he said, shaking hands with as many of them at once as he could, and hoping they hadn't come to say they'd found out about his losing the books, but feeling dreadfully scared in case they had.

'Nice weather,' said the Library man from SOUTH PAGWELL.

'And such a lot of it,' said the PAGWELL GARDENS man.

Then in came Mrs Flittersnoop with the tea.

After tea they started talking about things, and it wasn't long before they got round to the subject of Lobsters.

'I always say that Lobsters make better fathers than mothers,' said the UPPER PAGWELL man.

'Nonsense,' said the LOWER PAGWELL man, 'quite the other way about.'

'Let's look it up,' said the PAGWELL DOCKS man. 'The Professor's got a copy of "The Life and Likings of a Lobster," haven't you, Professor?'

'Certainly,' said the Professor. 'I'll fetch it. It's upstairs.'

He went upstairs and climbed out of his bedroom window. He slid down the drain pipe, got on the Colonel's bicycle, and pedalled away to the library at PAGWELL TOWN for all he was worth. The wheels flew over the ground, people flew out of the way, dust flew up

ALL THE FOURTEEN LIBRARY MEN CAME IN TO TEA.

all over the place, and the Professor's coat-tails flew out behind.

How the Professor pedalled ! How he panted and gasped, and how he hoped the library men wouldn't think he was too long getting the book.

At last—PAGWELL TOWN. The Professor swerved and missed a bus by half an inch. It was the only time he was glad to miss a bus. He fell off the bicycle, fell into the library, gasped for the book, snatched it, and was bicycling back almost before the assistant Library man had let go of the book.

Back up the drain pipe he crawled and came down trying to look quite calm, but with his breath going 'puff, puff, puff' inside him, like a steam engine.

All the Library men were looking at the books on his shelves.

' Here's the book, Professor,' said one of them, holding up a green volume ; ' you didn't leave it upstairs.'

' No, it's here,' said another, and another, and another, and all the Library men held up green books. They were all the copies of *The Life and Likings of a Lobster* that the Professor had lost.

Yes, they were on his own bookshelves all the time. You see, he couldn't find them because he'd put each one among a different class of books. One copy he put under ' Lobsters,' another he put under ' Biographies,' another under ' Deep Sea Fishing,' and another under ' How Much Do You Know ? ' Still another he had put under ' Folk Lore ' and one under ' Natural History,' and so on. And each time he'd looked for the book he'd looked on the wrong section of his bookshelves, and, not seeing it, hadn't bothered to look there again.

It was all very careless and complicated, but you see how it happened.

But it was all right now, and the Library men took their own books back with them, though they couldn't make out why the Professor wanted fourteen copies of the same book.

'He's very clever, I tell you,' said the PAGWELL CENTRAL man as they left the Professor's house. 'He probably reads them all at once in different chapters.'

BURGLARS !

THE PROFESSOR'S
MAGNETIC SUSPENDERS

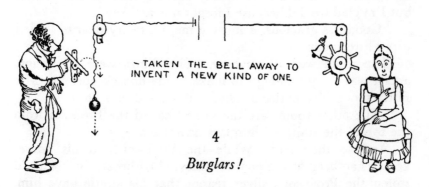

- TAKEN THE BELL AWAY TO INVENT A NEW KIND OF ONE

4

Burglars!

PROFESSOR BRANESTAWM rang the bell for his housekeeper, and then remembering that he'd taken the bell away to invent a new kind of one, he went out into the kitchen to find her.

'Mrs Flittersnoop,' he said, looking at her through his near-sighted glasses and holding the other four pairs two in each hand, 'put your things on and come to the pictures with me. There is a very instructive film on this evening ; all about the home life of the brussels sprout.'

'Thank you kindly, sir,' said Mrs Flittersnoop, 'I've just got my ironing to finish, which won't take a minute, and I'll be ready.' She didn't care a bent pen-nib about the brussels sprout picture, but she wanted to see the Mickey Mouse one. So while the Professor was putting on his boots and taking them off again because he had them on the wrong feet, and getting some money out of his money-box with a bit of wire, she finished off the ironing, put on her best bonnet, the blue one with the imitation strawberries on it, and off they went.

* * *

'Dear, dear,' said the Professor when they got back from the pictures, 'I don't remember leaving that window open, but I'm glad we did because I forgot my latchkey.'

'Goodness gracious, a mussey me, oh deary deary!' cried Mrs Flittersnoop.

The room was all anyhow. The things were all nohow and it was a sight enough to make a tidy housekeeper like Mrs Flittersnoop give notice at once. But she didn't do it.

'The other rooms are the same,' called the Professor from the top of the stairs. 'Burglars have been.'

And so they had. While the Professor and his house-keeper had been at the pictures thieves had broken in. They'd stolen the Professor's silver teapot that his auntie gave him, and the butter-dish he was going to give his auntie, only he forgot. They'd taken the Housekeeper's picture-postcard album with the views of Brighton in, and the Professor's best egg-cups that were never used except on Sundays.

'This is all wrong,' said the Professor, coming downstairs and running in and out of the rooms and keeping on finding more things that had gone. 'I won't have it. I'm going to invent a burglar catcher ; that's what I'm going to invent.'

'We'd better get a policeman first,' said Mrs Flittersnoop.

The Professor had just picked some things up and was wondering where they went. 'I'll get a policeman,' he said, putting them down again and stopping wondering. So he fetched a policeman, who brought another policeman, and they both went into the kitchen and had a cup of tea, while the Professor went into his inventory to invent his burglar catcher and Mrs Flittersnoop went to bed.

Next morning the Professor was still inventing. It was lucky the burglars hadn't stolen his inventory, but they couldn't do that because it was too heavy to take away, being a shed sort of workshop, big enough to get inside. They couldn't even take any of the Professor's inventing tools because the door was fastened with a special Professor lock that didn't open with a key at all but only when you squeezed some tooth-paste into it and then blew through the keyhole. And, of course, the burglars didn't know about that. They never do know about things of that sort.

'How far have you got with the burglar catcher?' asked Mrs Flittersnoop presently, coming in with breakfast, which the Professor always had in his inventory when he was inventing.

'Not very far yet,' he said. In fact, he'd only got as far as nailing two pieces of wood together and starting to think what to do next. So he stopped for a bit and had his breakfast.

Then he went on inventing day and night for ever so long.

'Come and see the burglar catcher,' he said one day, and they both went into his study, where a funny looking sort of thing was all fixed up by the window.

'Bless me!' said Mrs Flittersnoop. 'It looks like a mangle with a lot of arms.'

'Yes,' said the Professor, 'it had to look like that because it was too difficult making it look like anything else. Now watch.'

He brought out a bolster with his overcoat fastened round it and they went round outside the window.

'This is a dummy burglar,' he explained, putting the bolster thing on the window-sill. 'In he goes.' He opened the window and pushed the dummy inside.

Immediately there were a lot of clicking and whirring noises and the mangle-looking thing twiddled its arms. The wheels began to go round and things began to squeak and whizz. And the window closed itself behind the dummy.

4

'It's working, it's working,' cried the Professor, dancing with joy and treading on three geraniums in the flower-bed.

Suddenly the clicking and whizzing stopped, a trap-door opened in the study floor and something fell through it. Then a bell rang.

'That's the alarm,' said the Professor, rushing away. 'It means the burglar thing's caught a burglar.'

He led the way down into the cellar and there on the cellar floor was the bolster with the overcoat on. And it was all tied up with ropes and wound round with straps and tapes so that it looked like one of those mummy things out of a museum. You could hardly see any bolster or coat at all, it was so tied up.

'Well I never,' said Mrs Flittersnoop.

The Professor undid the bolster and put his overcoat on. Then he went upstairs and wound the burglar catcher up again, put on the Housekeeper's bonnet by mistake and went to the pictures again. He wanted to see the brussels sprout film once more, because he'd missed bits of it before through Mrs Flittersnoop keeping on talking to him about her sister Aggie and how she could never wash up a teacup without breaking the handle off.

Mrs Flittersnoop had finished all her housework and done some mending and got the Professor's supper by the time the pictures were over. But the Professor didn't come in. Quite a long time afterwards he didn't come in. She wondered where he could have got to.

'Forgotten where he lives, I'll be bound,' she said. 'I never did see such a forgetful man. I'd better get a policeman to look for him.'

PROF. BRANESTAWM TESTS
HIS BURGLAR CATCHING
MACHINE

·AND WENT TO
THE PICTURES
AGAIN·

But just as she was going to do that, ' br-r-r-ring-ing-ing-g-g '
went the Professor's burglar catcher.

' There now,' cried Mrs Flittersnoop.   ' A burglar and all.
And just when the Professor isn't here to see his machine
thing catch him.   Tut, tut.'

She picked up the rolling-pin and ran down into the
cellar.   Yes, it was a burglar all right.   There he lay on the
cellar floor all tied up with rope and wound round with straps
and tapes and things till he looked like a mummy out of a
museum.   And like the bolster dummy, he was so tied up you
could hardly see any of him.

' Ha,' cried the Housekeeper, ' I'll teach you to burgle,
that I will,' but she didn't teach him that at all.   She hit him
on the head with the rolling-pin, just to make quite sure he

shouldn't get away. Then she ran out and got the policeman she was going to fetch to look for the Professor. And the policeman took the burglar away in a wheelbarrow to the police station, all tied up and hit on the head as he was. And the burglar went very quietly. He couldn't do anything else.

But the Professor didn't come home. Not all night he didn't come home. But the policemen had caught the other burglars by now and got all the Professor's and the House-keeper's things back, except the postcards of Brighton, which the burglars had sent to their friends. So they had nothing to do but look for the Professor.

But they didn't find him. They hunted everywhere. They looked under the seat at the pictures, but all they found was Mrs Flittersnoop's bonnet with the imitation strawberries on it, which they took to the police station as evidence, if you know what that is. Anyhow they took it whether you know or not.

' Where can he be? ' said the Housekeeper. ' Oh! he is a careless man to go losing himself like that ! '

AND THE BURGLAR WENT
VERY QUIETLY

Then when they'd hunted a lot more and still hadn't found the Professor, the Judge said it was time to try the new burglar they'd caught. So they put him in the prisoner's place in the court, and the court usher called out ''Ush' and everybody 'ushed.

'You are charged with being a burglar inside Professor Branestawm's house,' said the Judge. 'What do you mean by it ?'

But the prisoner couldn't speak. He was too tied up and wound round to do more than wriggle.

'Ha,' said the Judge, 'nothing to say for yourself, and I should think not, too.'

Then the policeman undid the ropes and unwound the straps and tapes and things. And there was such a lot of them that they filled the court up, and everyone was struggling about in long snaky sort of tapes and ropes and it was ever so long before they could get all sorted out again.

'Goodness gracious me !' cried Mrs Flittersnoop, 'if it isn't the Professor !'

It was the Professor. There he was in the prisoner's place. It was he all the time, only nobody knew it because he was so wound up and hidden.

EVERYONE WAS STRUGGLING

'What's all this ?' said the Judge.

'Please, I'm Professor Branestawm,' said the Professor, taking off all his five pairs of glasses, which fortunately hadn't been broken, and bowing to the court.

'Well,' snapped the Judge. He was very cross because the

mixed-up tangle of tapes and things had pulled his wig crooked and he felt silly. 'What has that got to do with anything ? Didn't you break into the Professor's house ? '

'I left my key at home and got in through the window,' said the Professor, 'forgetting about the burglar catcher.'

'That is neither here nor there,' said the Judge, 'nor anywhere at all for that matter, and it wouldn't make any difference if it was. You broke into the Professor's house. You can't deny it.'

'No,' said the Professor, 'but it was my own house.'

'All the more reason why you shouldn't break into it,' said the Judge. 'What's the front door for ? '

'I forgot the key,' said the Professor.

'Don't argue,' said the Judge, and he held up Mrs Flittersnoop's bonnet that the Professor had worn by mistake and left under the seat at the pictures. 'This bonnet, I understand, belongs to your housekeeper.'

Mrs Flittersnoop got up and bowed. 'Indeed it does, your Majesty,' she said, thinking that was the right way to speak to a judge, 'but the Professor's welcome to it, I'm sure, if he wants it.'

'There you are,' said the Judge, 'she says he's welcome to it if he wants it. That means she didn't give it to him, did you ? "

'No,' said Mrs Flittersnoop, 'I thought . . .'

'What you thought isn't evidence,' snapped the Judge.

'Well, what is evidence, then ? ' said Mrs Flittersnoop, beginning to get cross, 'I never heard of the stuff. And I'm tired of all this talk that I don't understand. Give me my best bonnet and let me go. I've the dinner to get.'

'Oh, give the woman her bonnet,' said the Judge, and then he turned to the Professor.

'If it had been anybody else's house you'd broken into,' he said, ' we'd have put you in prison.'

'Of course,' said the Professor, trying on all his pairs of spectacles one after the other to see which the Judge looked best through.

'And if it had been anyone else who'd broken into your house, we'd have put him in prison,' said the Judge.

'Of course,' said the Professor, deciding that the Judge looked best through his blue sun-glasses because he couldn't see his face so well.

'But,' thundered the Judge, getting all worked up, ' as it was you who broke into the house and as it was your own house you broke into, we can only sentence you to be set free, and a fine waste of good time this trial has been.'

At this everyone in the court cheered, for they most of them knew the Professor and liked him and were glad everything was going to be all right. And the twelve jurymen cheered louder than anyone, although the Judge hadn't taken the least bit of notice of them and hadn't even asked them their verdict, which was very dislegal of him, if you see what I mean.

And as for Mrs Flittersnoop, she clapped her bonnet on the Professor's head, and then several people carried him shoulder-high out of the court and home, with the imitation strawberries in Mrs Flittersnoop's hat rattling away and the Professor bowing and smiling and looking through first one pair of glasses and then another.

THE SCREAMING CLOCKS

5

The Screaming Clocks

'I'M going to write some letters for half an hour and I'm not to be disturbed,' said the Professor to his housekeeper, arranging his five pairs of glasses nice and neatly on his forehead for when he wanted to use them, 'and I'll have a cup of tea when I've finished.'

'Yes, Sir,' said Mrs Flittersnoop, and she went into the kitchen to finish reading her book.

The clock on the mantelpiece said four o'clock as the Professor fastened the safety pins that he had on his coat because the buttons had fallen off, and sat down to write.

He wrote to his auntie and his cousin and his special friend. He wrote to the butcher by mistake about some cabbages, and he wrote to the Mayor about a nasty smell that seemed as if it might be drains but was really a disused bone that Mrs. Flittersnoop's sister's dog had pushed under the carpet. Then he wrote to the B.B.C. to say that someone was making squeaky noises on the wireless and to the laundry to say would they send back two buttonholes that were missing from his blue shirt.

'Only half-past four,' he said, looking at the clock. He had another half-hour to write letters and he'd written all his letters, so he thought for a bit and then wrote some postcards.

He wrote one to the Water Company to say that the water

came out of the taps twisted, and was this all right? He wrote
one to the coal people to say that the coal they sent was all
dirty. He sent a picture postcard of himself to his friend
Colonel Dedshott, of the Catapult Cavaliers, saying he could
come to tea on Sunday, and he sent one of Colonel Dedshott to
himself to remind him that he was coming and another to Mrs
Flittersnoop to remind her to get some crumpets because the
Colonel liked them.

Then he looked at the clock and it was still half-past four.

'Well, I must have written those postcards quickly,' he
said, looking at the clock through his long-sighted spectacles,
and he was just wondering what to write next when Mrs
Flittersnoop tapped at the door and came in with a cup of tea
and a nice big piece of cocoanut cake.

'Please, Sir, it's gone nine o'clock, and it's your bath
night,' she said.

'Don't be silly,' said the Professor, stirring his tea and
fishing out his near-sighted glasses that had fallen in. 'Look
at the clock, it's half-past four. It's been half-past four for
quite a long time.'

'There now,' said Mrs Flittersnoop, 'if the clock hasn't
stopped.'

'Well, if it hasn't stopped, what has it done?' said the
Professor, deciding not to have his bath after all, as it was so
late. 'There must be something wrong with it,' he went on,
forgetting to put sugar in his tea and wishing he'd remembered. 'I'll take it down to the clock-man when I go out to
the post.'

'I'll wrap it up for you, Sir,' said the Housekeeper, and she
took the clock out, leaving a dusty patch on the mantelpiece
where it had stood.

Presently the Professor finished his tea and went out into the kitchen to get the clock.

' What a nice tidy packet,' he said, picking up the parcel from the kitchen-table, and he was gone before Mrs Flittersnoop, who was in the middle of a chapter, could tear herself away and tell him he'd taken a bag of potatoes by mistake and that the clock was on the hall-stand.

When he got to the clock-man's shop it was shut, but the clock-man knew him, so he let him in.

' Please, this clock has stopped,' said the Professor. He put down the parcel, cut the string, and all the potatoes burst out, rolled across the counter and went bouncing and bobbing all over the floor.

' Dear me,' said the Professor, wondering whether clocks always turned into potatoes when they stopped and that, if so, how awkward it was.

' Seventeen little ones and six big ones,' said the clock-man, who had been crawling round the shop picking up the potatoes. ' Twenty-three all told. Is that all ? '

' I think there was another one,' said the Professor, who thought you bought potatoes in dozens. But there wasn't another one, so they didn't find it, even though they both looked through all five pairs of the Professor's spectacles one after the other.

' I'd better come back in the morning,' said the Professor, so the clock-man went to bed and the Professor went back with the potatoes and dropped absolutely several of them on the way.

Next day he took the stopped clock to the clock-man, who looked at it through a little spy glass, tapped it and turned it upside down, listened to it, smelt it,

-WARMED IT OVER
THE GAS -

scratched about inside it with a hairpin and warmed it over the gas.

'It wants winding up,' he said. 'That's why it stopped, and that will be fivepence-halfpenny.'

But the Professor hadn't listened to him any further than 'It wants winding up.' He was scratching his head with one finger and saying to himself: 'Wants winding up. Now why should it want winding up? Because it has run down. What one wants is a clock that doesn't run down and therefore doesn't have to be wound up. Someone ought to invent a clock like that. Invent . . . Ha! Who invents things? Professors do, of course, and aren't I a professor? Yes, I am, so I'll invent a clock that doesn't need winding up,' and he was just going to rush out of the shop when the clock-man caught him by the coat-tails.

'Here,' he said, 'while you're about it you might invent one of those clocks that don't run down for *me*, will you, and we'll say no more about the fivepence-halfpenny.'

So the Professor said all right, he would invent two clocks, one for himself and one for the clock-man, and he went off to invent them, saying no more about the fivepence-halfpenny.

*　　*　　*

It didn't take the Professor so long to invent the clocks

as he thought it was going to. In fact, it would have taken him less time still, only he found he'd run out of little weeney screws and had to send Mrs Flittersnoop out to buy a pennyworth.

On Sunday when Colonel Dedshott came to tea both the clocks were ready, even though he came immediately after breakfast. The Colonel always came to tea early, so as not to be late.

' And you mean to say those clocks will keep on going and telling the time right without ever being wound up,' said the Colonel, and he listened patiently while the Professor explained in awfully complicated language just how they worked. But he didn't understand a bit how they worked when the Professor had finished. He never could understand the Professor's inventions. They made his head go round and round so.

' Now we'll take one of the clocks down to the clock-man I promised it to,' said the Professor, putting on his golfing cap which he always wore on Sunday to save his proper week-day hat.

-THE PROFESSOR EXPLAINED-

' Hurray,' said the clock-man when he saw it. ' Thanks ever so, but I bet it runs down and has to be wound, all the same.'

' No, it won't,' said the Professor, ' not if you don't touch it. You see.'

So the clock-man said he'd see and he put it on the mantelpiece in his best parlour, taking away the dish of stuffed bananas that he used to keep there and putting them under the bath.

' Ta, ta,' said the Professor.

He raised his cap and all his spectacles fell off, but luckily none of them broke. The Colonel picked them up for him, saluted, clicked his heels and kissed his hand, and back they went, leaving the clock-man all excited to see if the clock would really go without winding.

*   *   *

The Professor and the Colonel were just having dinner together and the Professor was asking the Colonel to have a little more of everything to finish his lovely bread, when something happened.

The Professor's beautiful, marvellous and amazing never-stop clock went and struck thirteen !

' Coo,' said the Colonel with his mouth full, quite forgetting his manners he was so astonished. ' Is it meant to do that or has it got a pain in its cog-wheels ? '

' I shouldn't worry, sir, if I was you,' put in Mrs Flittersnoop, who had come in with a rice pudding. ' Clocks is funny things. I remember my sister Aggie had one that wouldn't go unless it was on its face, and then when it struck thirteen and the hands said a quarter to three you knew it was five o'clock.'

But the Professor was awfully upset. He wouldn't finish

his dinner and he walked up and down the room till he nearly wore the carpet out.

'Oh dear, let's run down to the clock-man and see if his clock has struck thirteen too,' he said at last, and he dashed out of the house without waiting to put his hat on or even to take his napkin out of his collar where he always tucked it in at meal-times.

When they got to the clock-man's he was all bothered and astonished too, because his clock had just struck fourteen.

'I see what I've done, yes I do,' shouted the Professor, while the clock-man was waving his arms and telling the Colonel that what he didn't know about clocks wasn't worth knowing, and that fourteen was a silly time for any clock to strike.

'I forgot all about the striking business,' went on the Professor, taking no notice of either of them. 'I've made the clocks so's they'll go for ever and never need winding and, of course, I've made them so's they go on striking for ever and not need winding. Only I forgot to put a little wiggly thing in, and instead of starting to strike one again after they've struck twelve, those clocks will go on striking thirteen, fourteen, fifteen and so on till they're striking goodness knows how many. Oh, dear,' and he sank wearily into a chair ; only the Colonel had just taken the chair to sit on, so he sat bump on the floor instead.

'But listen, this is awful,' he went on, getting all worked up but forgetting to get up. 'The clocks'll go on striking fifteen, sixteen, seventeen, eighteen, on and on.'

'And every hour they'll strike more and more,' put in the clock-man, just to show he knew all about clocks.

'And soon they'll be striking so many strikes that they

5

won't have time to finish striking one hour before it's time to begin striking the next. And what's going to happen then ? Oh dear,' cried the Professor. ' Oh, I must do something to the clock I've got, somehow, I must,' and getting up, he rushed back to his house again with the Colonel trying to keep up with him and the clock-man calling after him to hurry up and come back and do something to his clock, too.

When they got back there was a letter from the Water Company to say they didn't mind the water coming out twisted, but that if it came out in knots, to let them know. But the Professor didn't stop to read it. He dashed out into his workshop and came back with an armful of tools. Then he started trying to get the clock open.

He tried the screwdriver and the saw and he tried chisels, and he tried the tin-opener, but none of them was any good. Then he tried lots of tools of his own invention, but they weren't any good, either. For days and days he tried, and Mrs Flittersnoop got tired of waiting dinner for him and went to stay with her sister Aggie for a bit. Then the clock struck eighty-five, and in despair the Professor started biting it. But that wasn't any good either, and before long the never-stop clock was going dong, dong, dong, dong, dong, all the time without a pause.

' Oh dear, I'll never invent a clock again, no I won't,' gasped the Professor, now all tired out and weary.

Then there came a knock at the door, and the clock-man's little girl came in to say that father said their clock was humming.

' Humming,' said the Professor. ' Clocks don't hum. But, oh yes, of course. It's striking so many that it hasn't time to catch itself up and it has to keep on striking quicker and quicker, so it goes dong-ng-ng all the time.'

'Yes,' said the clock-man's little girl, 'that's just how it is going.'

'Go and tell your father to come and see me,' said the Professor, giving her a handful of nails in mistake for a handful of sweets. Then he went out into the garden to think.

But just as he was beginning to start getting ready to think there was a loud bang in the distance, and the next minute the clock-man dropped out of the sky right on to the calceolarias.

'Oh, you needn't have hurried so,' said the Professor, but the clock-man was waving his arms and trying to say everything at once. And his clothes were all torn and his face all dirty.

'The clock,' he managed to stammer out at last. 'It went bang. It started humming. It hummed and hummed and got shriller and shriller and then bang it went, and here I am.'

'Good heavens!' cried the Professor, clutching at a

IT WENT BANG

hollyhock to steady himself. 'Of course, it kept striking quicker and quicker to catch itself up, and the quicker it struck the shriller it would make it hum, and——' He stopped suddenly, for from the house came a shrill wailing screech. Weeeeeeee !

'The clock !' yelled the Professor. 'It's going to go bang, and my clock is a much bigger one than yours and if yours blew you all the way here, whatever will happen if my bigger clock goes bang ? '

They dashed into the house. The Professor dashed to the mantelpiece. He grabbed the screaming clock and dashed out of the window, forgetting to open it first and smashing the glass, bing ! all over the place.

Down the road he rushed, through Great Pagwell, past the ruins of the clock-man's house that his clock had blown up, and down to Lower Pagwell, with the clock shrieking and screeching and getting shriller at every stride. He passed Mrs Flittersnoop, who was on the way back to see if he was ready for dinner yet, but when she saw him and heard the clock, she went back to her sister Aggie's again.

Over the hedge dashed the Professor and down to the lake.

Screeeeech ! went the clock.

The Professor drew back his hand and hurled it as far as ever he could, which wasn't very far ; then he turned and rushed back.

Boom—whoosh—ploshety—bing ! The clock burst with a terrific crash and blew up so much water from the lake that everyone in Lower Pagwell got a bath although it wasn't bath night.

*   *   *

THE CLOCK BURST
WITH A TERRIFIC CRASH –

' I'm sorry about your house being all busted,' said the Professor to the clock-man, ' but I'll invent you a new one, shall I ? '

But the clock-man said he'd rather invent his own house, thank you all the same.

THE FAIR AT
PAGWELL GREEN

6

The Fair at Pagwell Green

DOWN at Pagwell Green everyone was all excited and
delighted. The grown-ups were getting out their best
clothes and the children were asking for pennies.
Caravans and things were going by, rumble, rumble,
bangetty bump, and people were shouting 'whoa' and
'gee up,' and motors were going chug, chug, pop, pop. For
a simply too gorgeously lovely Fair had arrived.

Soon there were tents all over the place and stalls all
over the place. And instead of people shouting 'whoa' and
'gee up' they were shouting 'Buy, buy, buy,' and 'Here you
are, sir, try your luck,' and 'Three shies a penny,' and 'All
you ring you have.' And instead of motors chugging and
popping there were roundabouts going tum-ti-tiddley-um-tum,
pompetty-om-pom, toot, toot. And people were buying and
trying their luck, and not ringing anything worth having, but
not caring anyway. The coco-nuts were being shied at and—
well you know what Fairs are like without being told, don't you?

The Fair was all going fine when Professor Branestawm,
who had been to see a friend at Great Pagwell, went by, and
saw it.

'Bless me now, a Fair!' said the Professor, stopping and
looking at it through his long-sighted spectacles. 'Well now, I
haven't been to a Fair since I wore short trousers. I think I'll go.'

-SUCH A DEAD SHOT·

So he went home for some money and called for Colonel Dedshott of the Catapult Cavaliers to go to the Fair with him. He would have taken Mrs Flittersnoop, his housekeeper, only she was staying away with her sister Aggie in Lower Pagwell.

' Hurray, I love Fairs,' said the Colonel, who was afraid the Professor had called to tell him about a new invention, but hoped he didn't, because the Professor's inventions made his head go round and round.

So off they went to the Fair and of course the Colonel being such a dead shot did the most extreme things. He knocked down all the coco-nuts and he ringed, or rang, whichever it ought to be, all the houp-la prizes, except a gilt teddy bear, which he didn't want much. And before long he had such a pile of clocks and boxes of this and that, and bottles of the best boiled sweets, to say nothing of dozens of coco-nuts, that he simply had to go and see about a cart to take them all home. And the Fair people weren't a bit pleased about it, because you aren't supposed to win all those things, no you aren't.

' I shall go and look at the waxworks,' said the Professor, and off he went.

*　　*　　*

Down in Lower Pagwell, Mrs Flittersnoop's sister was saying to her, 'Look here, Amelia, you don't get out much, I'll lend you my Sunday hat and my best feather boa and the black satin coat with the embroidery that my great-aunt Sarah gave me, and you get off and enjoy yourself at the Fair for a bit.'

'Well, I do think that's nice of you, Aggie,' said Mrs Flittersnoop, and off she went all dressed up in her sister's best things, feeling a frightful swell and looking most unexpected.

'There now, a waxwork show,' she said when she saw the big tent with 'Wigglepatch's Waxworks' printed on the side, 'now that's what I call something like. I don't hold with all these houp-la's and roundabouts and excitable things for a woman of my age. I'll just take a walk round the waxworks and then I'll go and have a nice cup of tea.' So in she went.

Inside the waxworks there were all sorts of figures of people of importance. There was even a waxwork of Professor Branestawm. Yes, and it was so much like him when he stood and thought, which he often did, that Mrs Flittersnoop thought it was really the Professor and said, 'Good afternoon, Sir, I hope I see you well.'

But, of course, the waxwork didn't answer, so Mrs Flittersnoop went on looking at the others and wondering if the Professor was annoyed with her or had got too proud to speak or what.

And while she was sitting on a seat, wondering, along came the Professor himself, who had been looking to see if there was a waxwork of Heath Robinson, but there wasn't. And Mrs Flittersnoop was sitting so still thinking that the Professor thought she was a waxwork.

'Now, who can this be, I wonder,' he said, peering through his near-sighted glasses because he didn't recognise her in her sister's best clothes. 'I wonder where the label is.'

'Label, indeed,' thought Mrs Flittersnoop, but she didn't say anything and she didn't move. She was beginning to get cross with the Professor. And the more he peered the more cross she got. 'What a funny waxwork,' he said at last and went away.

'Heavens, he thinks I'm a waxwork,' exclaimed Mrs Flittersnoop, when he'd gone. 'Bless me now, what can be the matter with the man. He's acting that strange he must be getting silly in the head. That's because of me not being at the house to look after him this past week, I'll be bound. I'd better go and tell Aggie it's time I went back to look after him.'

So out she went ; while the Professor was standing at the other side of the tent wondering who the waxwork could be that he thought Mrs Flittersnoop was.

He thought and he thought, but couldn't think of anything likely. And presently it was closing-time. Then the Waxwork man came round covering the waxworks with sheets. And the assistant Waxwork man came round helping him. And what do you think that silly assistant Waxwork man went and did ? Why, he threw a sheet over the Professor, thinking it was the waxwork of the Professor he was covering up. The real waxwork of the Professor had been covered up by the chief Waxwork man, but his assistant didn't know. And the Professor was so deep in thought he didn't notice, so there he was all covered up with a sheet and shut in with the waxworks. Oo-er !

*   *   *

' I must be getting along back to the Professor's now, dearie,' said Mrs Flittersnoop to her sister. ' The poor gentleman's got that funny since I've been away, there's no telling what'll be happening to him,' so she gave her sister back her best clothes, packed her box, and got along back to the Professor's.

While she was waiting for the Professor to come home from the Fair, she went into the kitchen to tidy up, expecting to find simply all the dishes and plates dirty, because the Professor didn't know anything about washing up, it was too ordinary. But there was only one plate dirty and that was the one the cat had.

' Bless me,' she said. ' The man's forgotten to eat.' But he hadn't. He'd been out to dinner and tea and everything with the man next door.

Soon it was ever so late and the Professor hadn't come home. So Mrs Flittersnoop, being all anxious, put on her ordinary things and went to find Colonel Dedshott.

' The Professor's at the Fair, Sir,' she said, ' and acting most strange, too. And he hasn't come home, so like as not he's got himself shut in the Waxwork Show ; you know what he is.'

' Of course,' said the Colonel, who had just finished counting the clocks and coco-nuts and things he'd won. ' We must go at once and even then we shall not get there till we arrive.'

So back they went, crawled under the flap of the Waxwork Tent and started looking for the Professor.

' Here he is,' said Mrs Flittersnoop. But it was the waxwork Professor they'd found, only they didn't know it. They thought he'd gone all stiff because he was thinking too hard, or that he'd gone to sleep or was frozen or something. And they carried out the Waxwork Professor between them and took it very carefully home.

*   *   *

No sooner had Mrs Flittersnoop and the Colonel gone out with the waxwork, than the real Professor Branestawm suddenly stopped thinking and found himself all covered up with a sheet.

'Tut, tut, I'm shut in with the waxworks,' he said.   'How

"HERE HE IS," SAID
MRS FLITTERSNOOP.

silly.' So he threw off the sheet, popped some toffee the Colonel had given him into his mouth and out he went.

But he hadn't thrown the sheet off at all, he only thought he had, and it was trailing along behind him with the words ' Wigglepatch's Waxworks ' painted on it as big as anything.

' Oh,' cried the two Waxwork men when they saw him come out of the tent. ' Help, a waxwork's come to life ! Ow, ah, terrible, awful ! ' and they ran off shouting, ' A waxwork's come to life ! ' while the Professor started trying to find the way out of the Fair, but he'd forgotten which way it was and got lost among the roundabouts.

' Help, murder, fire, wow ! ' shrieked the Waxwork men, running the opposite way and knocking over lots of ice-cream barrows. Bump—they ran into the Head Fair Man.

' What's all this ? ' he demanded, his big fierce moustache going all spiky. ' Waxwork come to life ? Wonderful ! Amazing ! What an attraction ! Catch it quick ! '

Soon the Waxwork men and the ice-cream men and the roundabout men were all chasing the Professor, who ran like anything because he thought they wanted to get him arrested for being in the Fair after closing-time.

Round and round the Fair they went. Down the water-chute, round the roundabouts, up the lighthouse and down the switchback, and at last they caught him just as he was trying to hide behind the Aunt Sally.

' Splendid ! ' cried the Head Fair Man, rubbing his hands, ' A live waxwork. That's great. Bring it along.'

The Professor struggled like anything, but he couldn't get away. He tried to say he wasn't a waxwork at all, but his teeth were stuck fast in the Colonel's toffee and he couldn't utter a sound.

So they took the poor Professor back to the Waxwork **Tent** and locked him in a spare cage that a performing bear used to be kept in.   Then they put up placards : ' This way for the wonderful living waxwork.   The only one of its kind.   Won-

derful attraction.   Admission sixpence.'   Then they all went home to bed.

' Oh dear, oh dear,' thought the Professor, for he still couldn't speak because of the toffee. ' Oh, this is awful. I'm all locked in and nobody knows it's me. Oh, whatever will happen to me, oh dear.'

*   *   *

At the Professor's house Mrs Flittersnoop and the Colonel were trying to get the Waxwork Professor to drink some hot broth. They had a hot-water bottle at his feet and one on his chest. And a fire in the room.

'He's not so stiff now,' said the Colonel. 'That means he's getting better.' Then Mrs Flittersnoop gave a scream.

'Oh, oh, oh!' she cried, 'Oh, look, the poor man's hand is melting.' And so it was. The hot broth and the hot bottles and the hot fire were too hot for the waxwork, and it was beginning to melt. That's why it wasn't so stiff.

'Heavens!' exclaimed the Colonel, making a mighty guess at what had happened and getting it right first time. 'It isn't the Professor at all, it's a waxwork of him! Quick, we must get it back before it's missed, or they'll send a policeman for us.'

So down to Pagwell Green they hustled as fast as they could go, which wasn't very fast, because the waxwork was heavy.

* * *

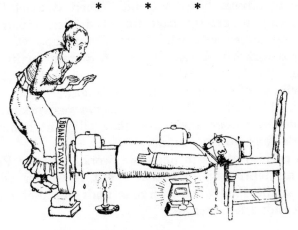

—IT WAS BEGINNING TO MELT

Inside the cage the Professor was in an awful state. He kept running round and round and up and down. He shook the bars of the cage ; he kicked them ; he bit them ; but he couldn't get out. He felt he was going mad. It was awful.

Then suddenly something came slithering under the edge of the tent.

' Heavens ! ' cried the Professor, for the toffee had come unstuck by now. ' It's me ! Then if that's me, I must be a waxwork after all. Oh, how awful. Oh, I shall never invent anything more. Hullo ! ' He said the last word in surprise, for Mrs Flittersnoop and the Colonel came wriggling under the tent as well and hauled the waxwork on to its feet.

' Hurray ! ' cried the Professor, dancing with joy and not biting the bars any more. ' I'm not a waxwork after all. That's the waxwork. How funny ! '

But they were too astonished at seeing the Professor in the cage to answer him for a bit. Then Colonel Dedshott started trying to get the cage unlocked with a pair of nail scissors and a pen nib, while Mrs Flittersnoop was holding up the waxwork which was still too soft to stand by itself.

At last the Colonel had the cage open and the Professor simply fell out of it and danced with delight.

' Quick ! ' cried the Colonel. ' Put the waxwork in.' Then he fastened the door again and they all went home to the Professor's house to have supper.

' I'm ever so glad I'm not a waxwork,' said the Professor, stirring his tenth cup of cocoa. ' But I wonder what will happen at the Fair when everyone finds out that the living waxwork isn't alive after all.'

THE PROFESSOR
SENDS AN INVITATION

-TO SEE
WHAT ON
EARTH HE
WAS DOING

The Professor sends an Invitation

FUNNY sorts of sounds were coming from Professor Branestawm's room. Mrs Flittersnoop, who wanted to ask him if he'd like his potatoes hard-boiled or mashed for dinner, stopped outside the door and didn't know whether she ought to disturb him.

Scratch, scratch. Popetty pop. Was he inventing something, or was it mice? Squeaky squeak. Did something need oiling or was the Professor trying to sing? Scratchety squeak. Very mysterious.

Mrs Flittersnoop made up her mind that she would disturb him if only to see what on earth he was doing. So she tapped on the door and went in, closing it very softly behind her so as not to disturb him very much.

Well, the Professor wasn't inventing anything and there were no mice. Nothing seemed to need oiling and the Professor wasn't singing. He was writing a letter and, as the pen was simply old and ancient because he'd forgotten to change the nib, it was going scratch, scratch, squeak as it went over the paper.

'Come in,' said the Professor, not realising that she was already in; so Mrs Flittersnoop, who was used to him and didn't want to get things muddled, went out again ever so softly and came in again to ask him about the potatoes.

'Oh, I think I'll have them mashed,' said the Professor, finishing his letter and forgetting to sign his name because he was thinking of potatoes.

'Very good, Sir, I'm sure,' said Mrs Flittersnoop, who liked them better boiled herself, but couldn't very well say anything. And out she went. Then the Professor took an envelope and addressed it to his friend Colonel Dedshott of the Catapult Cavaliers, Shoobangfire Cottage, Missfire Lane, Great Pagwell. It was a letter asking the Colonel to come to tea. The Professor was always writing to ask the Colonel to come to tea because he liked him, and the Colonel liked it and it made things jolly.

But whether the Professor was thinking of some sort of a kind of an invitation he was going to invent, or whether it was Mrs Flittersnoop popping in with questions about potatoes, or what it was, if anything, the Professor blotted his letter, folded the blotting-paper carefully and put it in the envelope and threw the letter away. Then he went out and posted that unlikely, silly, backwards sort of un-letter to the Colonel; and when he came back it was dinner-time, and he wished he'd asked for boiled potatoes instead of mashed ones, but anyway he liked chips better. Potatoes are silly.

*　　*　　*　　*　　*　　*　　*

The sun was gilding the tops of the houses in Great Pagwell as the postman went his rounds the next morning. He opened the gate of the Colonel's house with the Professor's letter in his hand. But the Colonel's special doggie was loose and came out and wuffed at him, so being a rather nervous sort of postman he stopped outside and tried to houp-la the letter through the letter-box. But he missed it by simply yards, and the letter sailed in through the window of the Colonel's bedroom, which he kept wide open all night because he was so military, and dropped on his nose, waking him up. But he was just to wake up anyway, so it didn't matter.

'Ha!' said the Colonel, 'letter for me. Good Heavens! where from?' He looked round the room and just then one of his ex-Catapult Cavalier butlers came in with an early morning cup of tea and a spoonful of cod-liver oil and malt, which the Colonel's auntie had made him promise to take.

'Did you bring this letter?' asked the Colonel, waving it about.

'No, Sir,' said the butler, putting the cup of tea on a table and the spoonful of cod-liver oil and malt into the Colonel's mouth according to orders. 'No letters have come this morning, Sir. Postman went by, Sir.'

-AND DROPPED
ON HIS NOSE -

' B-b-blug-a-glug-a-mmmmm,' said the Colonel. You know what cod-liver oil and malt is like, and this was even more so because it was some the Colonel's auntie had made herself, and she'd put some treacle in to make it taste nicer, which had made it much nastier.

' Glug-g-g-g-m-blug-m,' said the Colonel, then he swallowed the cod-liver oil and malt and got his talk back. ' But, good gracious, how can it be? Here is a letter, and you say letters haven't come. If the postman went by, how did this get here? ' He picked the letter up and waved it about again, making his tea rather cold.

' No letters came, Sir, and the postman went by, Sir,' said the butler again, and clicking his heels he saluted and went out, slamming the door slightly.

' Good gracious ! ' said the Colonel. He opened the letter.

' Good ever so much more gracious ! ' he exclaimed, turning the letter over and looking first at one side and then at the other. ' Strange letter that comes when postman goes by. Strange writing that I can't read. Oo-er, what can it be ? Is it message from secret society ? Can't be. I don't know any secret societies. Is it puzzle to be solved to win a motor-car and other handsome prizes ? '

But think as he might the Colonel couldn't think who his strange letter could be from. Because the Professor had sent him the blotting-paper he had blotted the letter with instead of the proper letter itself, all the writing was backwards and he couldn't read it. And it was a bit spready out and smudgy too, as blotting-paper always does make things, and that made it harder.

The Colonel got up and dressed, still thinking hard about the mysterious unlikely sort of letter. And he was thinking so hard about it he put his trousers on upside down and had the most unreasonable struggle getting right way up in them again.

'I give it up,' he said to himself as he cracked his fourth egg. He didn't guess about the blotting-paper, because he never used any. He always wrote in pencil, because he'd been walloped when he was little for upsetting the ink. 'I don't understand it at all,' he muttered. 'There's only one man who can understand funny sort of mixed-up things like this, and that's Branestawm. I'll go along and see him.'

Of course, if the Colonel had been as clever as he might have been, but wasn't, he might have guessed that the Professor was the only person likely to send funny mixed-up sort of letters like that. But, he was so busy think-ing how the Professor would be able to solve the strange language he thought it was written in that he simply didn't think about the Professor him-self having written it and done something silly with it. And besides, he didn't know about the nervous postman houp-la'ing it through the window, and couldn't understand how it had come to be on his bed.

—HE PUT HIS
TROUSERS ON
UPSIDE DOWN—

So along he went with it to the Professor.

' Ah ! good morning, Branestawm,' he said ever so heartily, partly because he'd had so many eggs for breakfast, and partly because he liked him. ' I have a little problem after your own heart. A mysterious letter written in a language quite unknown to me and delivered by some magical agency right on to my bed.'

' Now, now,' said the Professor, wagging one finger at him. ' What did you have for supper last night ? If you have read my treatise on the effects of third and subsequent helpings of trifle accompanied or not by third and subsequent glasses of ginger beer after ten o'clock, you may know something of the activities of the dream function of the . . .'

' No, no, no, no,' cried the Colonel, hoping to stop the Professor before his head began to go round and round as it always did when he started those learned sort of talks. ' I don't like trifle and I never drink ginger beer, and I haven't read your book ; I only use it as a paper-weight because it's nice and heavy. Look at this ! '

He handed the letter to the Professor, who rang for Mrs Flittersnoop, and asked for his five pairs of spectacles, found he had them on, rang again, ting-ting tr-r-r-ring ting, to tell her she needn't come. But Mrs Flittersnoop thought he was in an extra hurry or had got tangled up in a new invention or something, and came bursting into the room, wiping her hands on her apron, for she was in the middle of a Yorkshire pudding, or rather in the middle of making one.

' Yes ? ' said the Professor, forgetting he had rung for her because he had started to look at the Colonel's letter. Then thinking it was about potatoes again, he hurriedly said, ' Oh ! chips today, please.' And Mrs Flittersnoop said, ' Very good,

Sir,' and went back to her Yorkshire pudding, not knowing what he meant, but expecting that it didn't matter.

'Very strange,' muttered the Professor, looking at the letter through all his spectacles one after the other, then two at a time and then altogether. He turned it upside down and sideways and then, shutting one eye, he looked along the edge of it. The Professor knew fourteen different languages, including five he had invented himself, three of which nobody else could understand, one even he wasn't very sure of and one special one for talking to babies with, which everyone understood except babies. He'd forgotten all about writing to ask the Colonel to tea and didn't recognise the blotting-paper letter at all.

'Most strange,' he said, wriggling the paper about and smelling it and tasting it and listening to it. 'It isn't any language I know and I didn't think there were any others. Can't be Japanese, because that goes up and down and this goes sideways. It isn't Idiomatic Crashbanian, because that's written round the edges of the paper. Dear, dear.'

'Perhaps it wasn't meant for me and I got it by mistake,' suggested the Colonel brightly, but the Professor took no notice. He searched among his books. He looked up writing, and caligraphy, and scribbling, and foreign languages, and post-office regulations, but that didn't help. He found that writing meant the act of writing, and that scribbling meant to write without care, but what was the good of that? He found that letters could be sent for so many ounces for so much according to how far they were to go, but nothing was said about what they were about if they came through the window.

Suddenly he picked up his hat, put it on upside down by mistake, rushed out so that his hat fell off, grabbed another one from the hat-stand and dashed out with it in his hand, forgetting to put it on.

' Hi ! Come back ! Half a mo ! ' called the Colonel.

But the Professor didn't deal in ' mo's ' and hadn't any half ones, so he was nearly at the top of the road before the Colonel caught up with him, because being military he'd had to put his hat on very carefully in front of a looking-glass.

' Where '—puf—' go- '—puf—' -ing ? ' panted the Colonel, all out of breath as he caught up with the Professor.

' Li- '—puf—' -braries,' stuttered the Professor, even more out of breath than the Colonel, because not being military he wasn't so used to running never mind whether after or away from people.

' What are they ? ' asked the Colonel when they were comfortably seated on a tram that was going the wrong way only they didn't know it, because the Professor hadn't said which way he wanted to go.

' Libraries,' said the Professor, still going in and out a bit much because he hadn't got all his breath back quite. ' Look up more books, find out about writing, two penny ones.' The last bit was for the conductor, who gave them two tings on his punch arrangement and two striped tickets with holes in them.

Then the tram stopped.

' Great Pagwell Baths,' called the conductor, and the Professor got out before the Colonel could stop him. The Great Pagwell library was twopennyworth the other way. But the Professor was still thinking about the strange letter and walked straight into the Great Pagwell Baths, past the place where it says, ' Pay here,' without paying anywhere, and fell into the swimming-bath. But, luckily, it was empty and being cleaned out, so he just went a slight bong on the bottom of the shallow end and came out again quite dry.

'What a nuisance!' he said when the Colonel told him about coming the wrong way. 'Trams look so alike at both ends one can never be certain which way they're going when they're standing still. We had better go on to Lower Pagwell library.'

So they went on there, but it wasn't any good, partly because the Lower Pagwell library had only adventure sort of books, and books about football and cricket and sportish kind of things like that. And, anyway, the Professor had left the mysterious letter behind, so it wouldn't have been any good whatever kinds of books there were.

'Oh dear,' sighed the Colonel, who was getting tired of everything, especially the letter, and beginning to think that in a minute he'd wish he'd not said anything about it ; 'you are a one, you know, Branestawm. Excuse me saying it. You're just like a story.'

'Who's a story?' said the Professor slightly sharply. 'You know I always speak the truth. It isn't scientific not to.'

'Two twopenny ones,' said the Colonel, for they were in another tram by this time, the right one, because the Colonel had taken the Professor by the arm and pushed him on to it before he could think of other places to go and look up things that might be to do with the letter but more likely wouldn't.

* * *

'Well, well, well,' said the Professor, shaking his head from side to side, and scattering his five pairs of spectacles all over the place as he walked into his house with the Colonel. ' This is a mysterious business is this, this is it is, isn't it? I can understand your getting a letter by post and not being able to read it, because of it being written in fearfully bad writing, but then you would be sure to be able to read just a word here and there, so this isn't that. Then I can understand your getting a letter by post written in some strange sort of language you couldn't understand, because it might have come to you by mistake instead of going to the strange sort of person it was meant for. But this isn't that either, because I can read at least some of all strange sorts of language and I can't read any of this one except the full stops, and they may be commas when they're translated.'

' Yes,' said the Colonel, who'd thought all that out by himself but didn't like to say so in case it sounded like swank. ' But this letter didn't come by post. It was just there when I woke up, and goodness knows why. It can't be a warning from a secret society who're going to do something nasty to me, because they wouldn't send a warning I can't read.'

' Perhaps they did though,' said the Professor, brightening up. ' Perhaps they wrote the warning in words that don't exist just to make it harder so that you couldn't read them and couldn't do what they're warning you to do so that they'd be sure to be able to do something nasty to you. Secret sort of societies like doing nasty things to people, I believe.'

' Oo—er,' thought the Colonel, but he was far too military to say it. The inside of him began to feel rather funny, as if he'd eaten too much plum pudding, or not enough porridge, or the wrong sort of mushrooms.

Just then came a loud tap at the door. The Colonel

grasped the Professor's hand with one hand and the poker with the other. If this was the secret sort of society come to do something nasty to him he would at least show them the sort of stuff Catapult Cavaliers were made of. Not that he knew exactly what they were made of, though the Professor most certainly did. But what did that matter when secret societies were at the door ?

Tap, tap, tap.

' C-c-c-c-c-come i-i-i-i-n-n-n,' stammered the Professor, feeling all nervous, not because he thought it was the secret society, but because he thought the Colonel had gone a bit silly and was going to hit him with the poker.

The door opened slowly and silently. The Colonel gripped the poker harder. The Professor wished he had his spectacles to look through, but he'd scattered them all in the hall shaking his head so much, and had forgotten to pick them up.

IT CARRIED SOMETHING
BEFORE IT

Through the door came a figure. It was small, it carried something before it. It came straight to the Professor. It was Mrs Flittersnoop's sister's little girl Connie bringing the Professor and the Colonel a cup of tea each. And on the tray by the cups were the Professor's five pairs of spectacles arranged in order ready for him to put on.

' Ah ! thank you, my dear,' said the Professor, putting his spectacles on in the wrong order, and some of them upside down, while the Colonel, feeling rather silly, began to poke the fire, which made him look even sillier than he felt because it was a gas fire.

' Cup of tea,' said the Professor, stirring his with the wrong end of the spoon.

' Ta,' said the Colonel, feeling he could do with one.

Mrs Flittersnoop's sister's little girl, who always liked coming to the Professor's house because there were such strange things there, saw the mysterious blotting-paper sort of letter on the table and picked it up.

' Oo—oh ! ' she said. ' Looking-glass writing.' She went across to the mantelpiece, climbed on a chair and held the paper to the mirror. But before she could read a word the Colonel and the Professor had it out of her hand and were both trying to hold it up to the mirror themselves, so that it nearly got torn to bits.

' Wait a minute,' said the Professor. ' I see what it is. It's an invitation. It's from someone asking someone else to come and have tea with them to-day.'

' But, who's it from ? ' cried the Colonel, getting most excited because he liked going out to tea.

But they couldn't see that it was from the Professor because he'd forgotten to sign the letter, and they couldn't see that it was really for the Colonel because the ink had dried on the top part of the letter before the Professor had blotted it, and it hadn't come out on the blotting-paper.

' Ha, ha ! how funny,' cried the Colonel. ' Fancy writing to ask someone to tea in looking-glass writing so that they couldn't read it, and then sending it to the wrong person—that being me,' he added. ' Whoever it is wrote that letter must be a one, mustn't he or she ? '

' Yes,' said the Professor, thoughtfully turning the paper over in his hand. ' He or she must. But this gives me an idea. Why not stay and have tea with me ? I meant to write and ask you and forgot.' Of course he'd remembered really, but he'd forgotten he'd remembered and wanted to make sure he didn't forget. Professors are like that sometimes. It's because they know such a positive mound of important things they just can't possibly remember all the hundreds of little not important things.

' I'd love to,' said the Colonel. So Mrs Flittersnoop laid them a nice tea in the dining-room with two sorts of bread and butter and four sorts of cake, two of which she'd made herself from a recipe her sister Aggie had cut out of the *Lower Pagwell Weekly Gazette*.

' Well,' said the Colonel, passing his plate for his fifth piece of cake, ' somebody wrote to somebody to ask him or her to tea today and the wrong person got it, but two other somebodies are having tea, so what does it matter ? '

' What, indeed,' said the Professor, pouring the tea into the sugar basin by mistake.

' Wouldn't it be funny if it was you who wrote that looking-glass sort of letter and sent to me and forgot all about it ? ' said the Colonel.

7

'Ha, ha!' laughed the Professor, 'wouldn't it just be too funny for anything?' and they laughed like anything to think how funny everything would have been if it had been what it actually was, though neither of them knew it.

THE PROFESSOR
STUDIES SPRING CLEANING

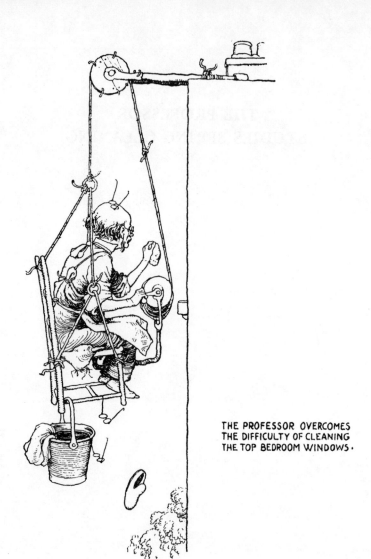

THE PROFESSOR OVERCOMES
THE DIFFICULTY OF CLEANING
THE TOP BEDROOM WINDOWS.

8

The Professor studies Spring Cleaning

PROFESSOR BRANESTAWM was having his breakfast in the bathroom. Of course, that was the sort
of thing Professor Branestawn was always rather likely
to do, through thinking about professorish sorts of
things instead of about breakfastish sorts of things. But that
wasn't the reason this time. Mrs Flittersnoop, his housekeeper, had started spring cleaning, and all the other rooms
were being turned out.

  ' Spring cleaning is silly,' said the Professor to himself,

spreading marmalade on the sponge and wondering why it tasted funny. 'I must speak to Mrs Flittersnoop about it, I must.'

Just then Mrs Flittersnoop came in to see if he wanted some more toast, and was just in time to stop him trying to crack a piece of soap instead of his egg.

'Begging your pardon, Sir,' she said, 'but I was wondering if you'd be going out rather earlier this morning, as I'd like to be getting on with the cleaning like so as to get it done with, if I might make so bold.'

'Not at all,' said the Professor, pouring himself out a cup of tea, but pouring it into the bath by mistake instead of into his cup, so that it all ran away goggle goggle, uggle oof, down the waste pipe. 'That is to say, of course, yes, yes, I'll be getting along now.'

He took a bite out of a rather crisp piece of toast which burst into crumbs all over him, and went downstairs.

Downstairs was all full of furniture, for all the rooms were being turned out at once, so that everything was everywhere, with one or two things left over.

'Dear me,' said the Professor. He'd forgotten about the spring cleaning on the way downstairs, and he thought he must have walked into a furniture shop or something.

'I'll take this,' he said, picking up a chair that he rather fancied. It was the one he always sat in when he wanted to think, so no wonder he rather fancied it. 'Just wrap it up for me, will you.'

'Yes, Sir,' said Mrs. Flittersnoop, who had come down-stairs behind the Professor. She hadn't the least idea why he wanted his chair wrapped up, but the Professor often wanted things done she had no ideas about, so she just took the chair and wrapped it up as best she could, which was very badly, and left most of the chair showing.

' Er, thank you,' said the Professor, looking at her over the top of two pairs of glasses and underneath the other three pairs.

SOME – THOUGHT HE WAS TAKING IT TO MEND

Then picking up the chair he went out in his slippers, because he'd forgotten to change into his boots, and got on a bus to go and see his special friend Colonel Dedshott of the Catapult Cavaliers. But he had the most severe sorts of trouble with the chair on the bus, which was nearly full. Some of the people thought he had stolen it. Some of them thought he was taking it to mend, because what they could see of it sticking out of the wrapping certainly looked as if a few spots of mending wouldn't hurt it.   Others thought he wanted to sell it and buried their noses in their newspapers or stared at the advertisements in the bus or pretended to be looking for their handkerchiefs, in case he should ask any of them to buy it.   One rather large gentleman, who'd been standing fourpennyworth already and was getting tired, thought he'd brought it on for him to sit on.   So he sat on it and the Professor got off at the top of the Colonel's road and forgot all about the chair, which had goodness knows how many pennyworths of free ride and finished up in the Lost Property Office.

'Ha !' said the Professor, as he rang the bell.   'Dear old Dedshott.   Quite a time since I saw him.   Must ask him round to tea.'

Just then the Colonel himself opened the door, because his two butlers, ex-Catapult Cavaliers, were out in the garden beating a carpet with the rolling-pin and a coal shovel.   Professor Branestawm was busy at the moment writing down a note on his cuff to ask the Colonel to tea, and he walked straight in without seeing the Colonel at all.   And the Colonel, not being used to opening doors himself, had opened it right back on himself and was trying to get away from the coat and the hat pegs which were sticking into him slightly.   So he didn't see the Professor come in.   They hunted about for each other all over the place, but as the Colonel didn't know it was the Professor who had called, the Professor had to do most of the real looking.

At last they ran into each other, back to back, outside the coal shed.

'Ah ! my dear Dedshott,' said the Professor, holding out

his hand to shake hands, with the pencil he had been making notes with still in his fingers.

'Branestawm,' said the Colonel, in a warm sort of voice, for he was glad to see the Professor. He gripped the pencil by mistake for the Professor's hand. The Professor let it go, put his hand in his pocket and said, ' Can you lend me a pencil ? ' took his own out of the Colonel's hand, forgot what he was making notes about anyway, and they both went inside to have a glass of something.

'You must excuse things being so messed up,' said the Colonel, after they had had two cups of something, because the Colonel couldn't find the glasses, ' we're spring cleaning, and some of the rooms are being turned out. It's an awful nuisance,' he went on, ' having to turn all the things out of a room and then turn them all back again. Why don't you invent a machine that will do it ? '

'What say ? ' asked the Professor, who had been trying to work out how many times 3785 went into $8978756453645263555\frac{7}{8}$ or something on the tablecloth, but had come to the edge before he had finished.

'I say, why don't you invent a machine to turn rooms out and then turn them back again,' said the Colonel, getting out the laundry book and adding ' one tablecloth ' to the other things on the week's list. ' It would make things so nice and easy.' The Colonel understood all about domestic things like that. He could even mend his own socks, though he never did.

'Wait a minute,' said the Professor, excitedly emptying the Colonel's cup instead of his own, which was already empty, and starting to think like anything. ' I see what you mean. A sort of machine or engine of some kind connected as to its differentials by a crank operating in inverse ratio to——'

'Yes, yes,' cried the Colonel, not understanding any of what the Professor was saying, but knowing he'd go on and on until his head went round and round, which he didn't want it to do. 'I think you have the idea all right.'

But Professor Branestawn wasn't listening to the Colonel. He'd started to invent his spring-cleaning machine and nothing else mattered, not even if it did. He forgot about the Colonel, he forgot he was in the Colonel's house and not in his own, and started taking a clock to pieces to get out some special kind of little cog-wheels he wanted for his machine.

So while the Professor was busy with his inventing, the Colonel thought he would slip over and tell Mrs Flittersnoop not to bother with any more spring cleaning, as the Professor's machine would do it all for her as soon as he got it invented, which probably wouldn't be very soon, but never mind. Well, he certainly slipped over all right, but that was because he trod on a piece of orange peel, and by the time he got to the Professor's house the cleaning was all done and the furniture all back in its place, except the chair the Professor had taken away ; that was still at the Lost Property Office.

'Well,' said Mrs Flittersnoop, when she heard about what the Professor was doing, 'that will be nice I'm sure, not having to turn the rooms out. A thing I never could abide. And seeing as how the Professor's staying with you, Sir, as it were, perhaps you'd be so kind as to give him his boots, Sir, which same he left behind him this morning.'

'Oh—er, yes, not at all, certainly,' said the Colonel, taking the boots in one hand and raising his hat with the other. 'Er —good day.'

'Good day to you, Sir, I'm sure,' beamed Mrs Flittersnoop. 'Such a nice gentleman,' she said to herself as she went back to the kitchen to send a note to her sister Aggie to say she'd stay with her for a bit, which she always did when the Professor was away, for company or something.

* * *

'Good Heavens!' exclaimed Colonel Dedshott when he got back to his house. 'Whatever has happened? Accident? Explosion? Awful, terrible, oh dear!' The house was in a simply extreme muddle. Everything was everywhere except a few things that seemed to be nowhere. The piano was upside down in the coal cellar. The dining-room chairs were in the garden. The large picture of the Colonel in his Catapult Cavalier's uniform was all in bits, thank goodness, for it looked awful. Some of the carpets were up the chimney, and one chimney, at least, seemed to be all over the carpet. The gas cooker had a knot in the middle of it, and the best silver was wrapped in the spare-room mattress.

'Oh! my goodness me and all,' wailed the Colonel coming all un-military at seeing his nice house all over the place.

TAKING THE BOOTS IN ONE HAND & RAISING HIS HAT WITH THE OTHER

'What has happened, and why and how? Shall I go and fetch the police or the fire brigade or the old iron man or what?' He rushed into room after muddled-up room looking for the Professor, but couldn't find him. He found a chair just inside the kitchen door by falling over it. He found that the bath had got turned inside out, and when he struck a match to be able to see better, he found a slight escape of gas, and *voila!* down came considerable ceiling. But the Professor was nowhere to be seen.

The Colonel was just going to rush out screaming when something dark and dirty, and wearing five pairs of spectacles, issued from the umbrella stand. It was Professor Branestawm. Good gracious !

' I fancy some of my calculations were a little inaccurate, my dear Dedshott,' he said. ' I just had the machine nearly finished and something went sort of whiz and here I am.'

' Yes, I see you am—I mean, are,' said the Colonel, ramming his hands into his pockets so hard he burst clean through the bottoms of them, and sent fivepence halfpenny and four bulls-eyes spinning all over the floor. ' But here you don't stay. You just go home and invent your own house to bits, will you. I ought to have known better than let you stay here alone after what happened to the clock-man's house over the never-stop clock.'

' I—er, I—er,' began the Professor.

' Yes, I know you err,' said the Colonel, getting all clever for a moment. ' That's just the trouble. Go home and err there, that's a good chap.'

So the Professor went home and got there just at the same moment as a man from the Lost Property Office who had found some papers with the Professor's address in the stuffing of the lost chair, and had brought it back. So he gave the man his hat and left twopence on the hall-stand instead of the other way round. But the man was a bit quick-witted through doing crossword puzzles, and he changed them over, otherwise the Professor's hat might have gone into the Lost Property Office.

Then the Professor had a nice hot wash and started inventing the spring-cleaning machine all over again, while the
Colonel had men and people in to put things right. It cost
him an awful lot, but, fortunately, the Colonel had simply
pyramids of money left him by some fancy aunties or someone, so it didn't matter very much.

*   *   *

At last the machine was finished, but not before several
entirely unreasonable things had happened, such as the
Professor forgetting what he was inventing and turning it into
a new kind of mangle that would do nearly everything except
mangle, and then getting caught up in bits of invention and
having to shout for Mrs Flittersnoop to get him out, which,
fortunately, she was able to do because she had come back
from her sister's and she did knitting a lot and understood
tangles.

'There you are,' said the Professor to Colonel Dedshott,
whom he had asked over for tea to see the machine. 'No more
bother with spring cleaning. You just push this button and
pull that lever and twiddle these wheels, one one way and one
the other, then, at the same time, you lift this up here and pull
that and adjust the——'

'Lovely,' said the Colonel hurriedly before his head began
to go round and round as it always did when the Professor
started explaining things. 'Let's have a go with it.'

They carried it upstairs and put it in one of the rooms.

'Now when I start it,' said the Professor, 'it will turn
everything out of the room, and then clean all the dust out without us doing anything. You watch.'

He twiddled and pulled and pushed and turned and lifted
up this, that, and the other.

'Bz-z-z-z-z-pop, bang, chug-a-chug,' went the machine, and they ran out to watch it work.

'Pop, pop, bang-a-chug, bz-z-z-z, whizz, squeeeeeeeow, pop,' went the machine.

The Professor, the Colonel, and Mrs Flittersnoop ran out and stood in rows in the garden.

'It isn't going to work,' snorted the Colonel, wondering if it was tea-time yet.

Just then a nicely rolled-up carpet came sailing out of the window and fell on him.

'Ah !' said the Professor, and then a bed fell on him. A wardrobe missed Mrs Flittersnoop by inches, goodness knows how many, but it didn't matter because it was a special one of the Professor's own invention and made of rubber, so it wouldn't have hurt anyway.

'There you are,' said the Professor, coming out from under the bed just in time to be hit by a pillow. 'What did I say ? There's your spring cleaning being done, Mrs Flittersnoop.'

'Indeed it is, Sir,' said Mrs Flittersnoop, getting behind a bush in case any more wardrobes were coming. 'Wonderful, I call it, these things coming out like that.'

Soon everything that had been in the room was in the garden, but still the machine went on popping and clicking and whizzing.

'I'll go and stop it,' said the Professor. He ran upstairs and the next minute he came sailing out of the window and landed in the geranium bed, but, fortunately, all the geraniums had been scratched up the week before by Mrs Flittersnoop's sister's dog who was staying with them.

'Stop it !' gasped the Professor, with his mouth full of geranium bed.

' I'll stop it,' shouted the Colonel, and in he ran followed by Mrs Flittersnoop and the next-door man who had come over the fence to see what was doing.

The next minute they all came out of the window together and fell on the special rubber wardrobe which burst with a slight pop, scattering the Professor's spare socks, some books, a pot of jam, a small saw, a half-invented clockwork draught-board, but no men, and a piece of toffee that the Professor had kept there.

' Gracious,' gasped the Professor, rushing round the geranium bed, which, luckily, happened to be a round one. ' I see what it all is, I do. That machine was made to turn things out of a room and it keeps doing it. Whenever anyone goes in to stop it, it turns them out. What can we do, good gracious, don't ask me.'

' But, it must be stopped,' shouted the Colonel, and in he dashed again, but out he came again. Seven times he tried to stop that awful machine and seven times it threw him out. The geranium bed was full of dents.

The Professor fetched all the Great Pagwell Police, but the machine threw both of them out. He got the Fire Brigade, the Gas Company, and the Pagwell Borough Council, and it threw them out, all except the Mayor of Pagwell who hadn't come in case it wasn't dignified.

' Oh dear ! oh dear ! ' groaned the Professor, getting all his five pairs of spectacles so mixed up that he was seeing long-sighted sort of things through his near-sighted glasses. ' Oh ! I don't believe I'll ever invent anything else if I can remember not to.'

' Look here,' said the Colonel, ' we can't let that thing go on chugging and whizzing and throwing people out like that.

Something absolutely has got to happen about it and happen soon, I tell you.'

Just then something did happen about it. The machine itself came out of the window and fell with such a rattle in the geranium bed that three crocuses came up long before their time.

'Heavens!' gasped the Professor, guessing what had happened, because he knew more about the machine than the others, but not much more. 'It's turned itself out, so it has.'

'Well, I never,' said Mrs Flittersnoop, but nobody minded whether she ever or not. They were all too busy looking at the machine and saying things they didn't understand themselves to show how clever they were.

'Now,' said the Professor, 'I will show you how the machine puts things right after turning everything out of the room including all the dust and itself.'

He pulled a pushed lever. He untwiddled a twiddled wheel and he left several other things alone. Immediately the machine rose in the air and went back through the window.

'See!' cried the Professor, dancing about with excitement, 'now it will take the things back.' Which that wonderful machine proceeded to do. The bed and the chairs and the carpet and all the other things went sailing back through the window.

'Wonderful!' gasped everyone, but the next minute they none of them knew where they were until they all found themselves packed into the rather small room in which the machine stood.

'Help!' shouted the Professor from between three firemen, Colonel Dedshot, and two Borough Councillors. 'It's turned us in.'

— THEY · NONE OF THEM
KNEW WHERE THEY WERE ·

8

It certainly had and it didn't stop there, for in through the window came clouds of dust, half-bricks, bushes, pieces of this and that.

' Stop ! stop ! ' shrieked the Professor, as everyone rushed for the door and got stuck half-way. ' It'll bring the whole of everything here in a minute.'

Suddenly there was a crash and things stopped coming in. The garden roller had come in with the other things and landed right on the machine, smashing it to bits.

With a last despairing chug the spring-cleaning machine was finished.

' Thank goodness for that,' said everyone, mopping their foreheads with one another's handkerchiefs which they'd taken from one another's pockets by mistake because they were so crowded up.

They got themselves sorted out at last and went outside while Mrs Flittersnoop made cups of tea. Then everyone went home, feeling that a good, if exciting, time had been had by all.

Mrs Flittersnoop had to do all the spring cleaning over again because of the mess the machine had brought in. But the Professor let her have her sister Aggie's two aunties in who were both very good at cleaning, so it didn't take so long.

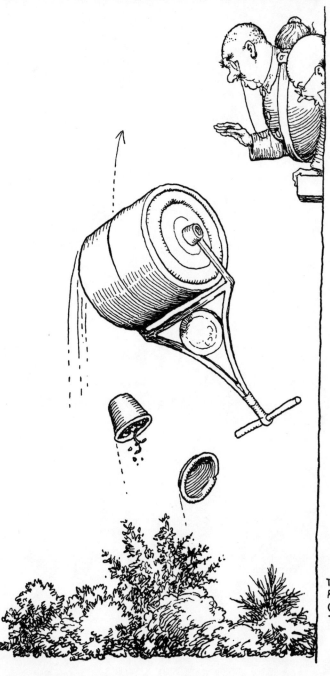

THE GARDEN
ROLLER HAD
COME IN WITH
THE OTHER
THINGS —

THE TOO-MANY PROFESSORS

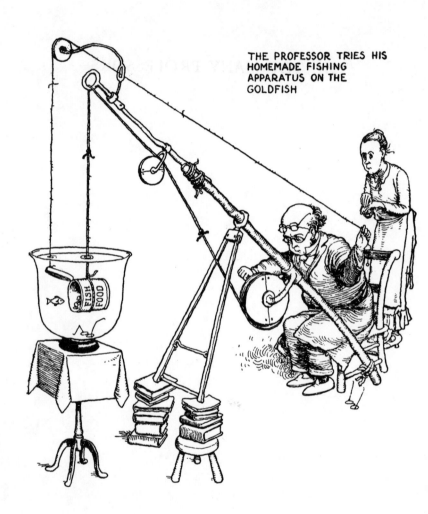

THE PROFESSOR TRIES HIS
HOMEMADE FISHING
APPARATUS ON THE
GOLDFISH

9

The Too-Many Professors

'LOR' bless my heart, whatever can that awful smell be?' gasped Mrs Flittersnoop, coming out of the kitchen all of a dither, with a smudge of flour on her nose because she was making cakes and her hair all over the place because she was making haste. 'Can't be the drains, for the man was here only yesterday to see to them. Can't be something gone bad, for I turned out the larder with my own hands this very morning.'

Sniff, sniff, pw-o-o-ugh—it certainly was an extreme sort of smell. Much worse than drains, not so bearable as something gone bad, utterly unlike any kind of smell anyone has ever smelt.

'It's the Professor I'll be bound,' said Mrs Flittersnoop, wiping her hands on her apron.

And it certainly was the Professor, for before Mrs Flittersnoop had time to get to the door of his inventory out he burst with a little bottle in one hand, a garden syringe in the other, and his clothes stained all the colours of the rainbow and some more besides.

'Amazing! astounding!' he shouted, pushing Mrs Flittersnoop aside, dashing into his study and then coming back to fetch her in as well.

'Begging your pardon, Sir, but if it's illegible spirits you're making I must give notice,' she said, putting her hands on her hips where they slipped off again because she was a bit thinnish.

'Listen,' gasped the Professor getting his five pairs of spectacles so mixed up that he could see four Mrs Flittersnoops all different sizes and one upside down. 'World will resound with discovery. Name a household word. Branestawm's bewildering bacteria, the secret of life revealed! I never used to think I was as clever as I thought I was, but now I see I'm much cleverer than I dared to hope I might be.'

Mrs Flittersnoop didn't answer. The Professor had just uncorked the bottle and the simply awful smellish odour immediately became so bad she had to bury her nose in her apron which unfortunately only buried half of it, because it was a long nose and a short apron.

'This liquid,' said the Professor, all of a tremble with excitement, 'will bring to life any picture to which it is applied. Look at this.'

He poured some of the sparkling liquid into a glass jar, drew some up in the syringe and squirted it over a picture of some apples on the cover of a book. Nothing happened, except that the picture got wet.

'Very good, Sir, I'm sure,' said Mrs Flittersnoop in a muffled sort of voice from inside the apron. 'And now I must be getting back to my cakes.' She was out of the room and half-way to the kitchen before the Professor could stop her and drag her back.

'Wait, wait, wait, wait,' he shouted excitedly. 'It takes time. Look, look!' he pointed with a quivering finger at the picture.

"Oo—er,' said his housekeeper. 'It's going all lumpy like.'

It certainly was. The apples began to swell up, the picture went all nobbly. Green smoke rose from the paper. The smell would have got worse only it couldn't. Then suddenly four lovely rosy apples rolled out of the picture on to the table, as real and solid as you please.

'Oh my!' exclaimed Mrs Flittersnoop.

'Try one,' said the Professor, and together they munched the apples. And except for a rather papery flavour and a funny feeling they gave you as if you were eating an apple in a dream that wasn't there at all but only seemed to be, the apples were certainly a success.

'It is rather a pity,' said the Professor, spraying a picture of a box of chocolates to life, 'that it costs more to make the liquid for doing this than it would cost to buy the things.'

"You don't say!" said Mrs Flittersnoop, taking a handful of the chocolates and not bothering about her cakes any more, which had burned themselves into cinders in the meantime, only neither of them could smell them because of the other smell, and thinking the Professor could just spray a few cakes out of a book if he wanted them.

'Yes,' said the Professor, hunting about among his books and papers, 'and there are certain limitations to the power of the liquid. The things it brings to life go back as they were when the liquid dries off.'

'Oo—er,' said Mrs Flittersnoop, thinking of the apples and chocolates she had eaten. But the Professor was pulling out a book with a picture of a cat in it.

'Let me try this,' he said, 'I don't know yet whether it will work with animals or people.'

He filled the syringe again while Mrs Flittersnoop hid behind the door in case the cat was a scratchy sort of one, which it was quite likely to, because most of the Professor's books were about wildish kinds of animals.

' Phiz-z-z-z-,' went the spray. They waited, the paper bulged, the picture smoked, the smell didn't get worse, just as before. Then—' Meow ! '—out jumped the cat.

But oh good gracious and heavens above, the next minute with a terrific whoosh of a zoom the whole room was full of an elephant !

' Amazing ! ' gasped the Professor, struggling out of the waste-paper basket where the elephant had knocked him. But Mrs Flittersnoop slammed the door and rushed screaming all the way to her sister Aggie's in Lower Pagwell without even stopping to wipe the flour off her nose.

The cat jumped out of the window and followed her, still meowing because the picture of it had showed it meowing and it didn't seem to be able to stop. But most definitely awkward of all, the elephant squeezed its big self through the french windows and followed her too.

' Heavens ! ' gasped the Professor, getting so worked up that

—HE DASHED AFTER THE ELEPHANT WHO SEEMED—

his socks came down. And he dashed after the elephant, dropping his glasses all over the place and holding his handkerchief hoping to be able to catch it and dry the wonderful liquid off it and make it go back into a picture, but not hoping so very much.

*   *   *

But while the Professor was chasing the elephant who was running after the cat who seemed to want to catch up with Mrs Flittersnoop, who definitely did want to get to her sister Aggie's, the most absolute things were going on in the Professor's room. Voices could have been heard if there had been anyone about to hear them. Rumblings and rustlings were occurring. Chatterings went up. People started talking round the place like goodness knows what.

When the elephant had come out of the picture so suddenly he'd upset the jar of wonderful liquid all over the Professor's photograph album. Good gracious, what a thing to do! Liquid that could make things come to life and all! And upset on a photograph album of all places!

TO WANT TO CATCH UP WITH MRS FLITTERSNOOP. —

When the Professor, who had given up the chase at Pagwell Gardens, came staggering back all out of breath the first thing he noticed was himself opening the door to himself.

'Good afternoon,' said the Professor, not recognising himself.

'Don't take it for a moment, the sun's in my eyes,' said the other one of him.

The Professor was just wondering what the answer to that

was when two more of himself, one at sixteen and one at twenty-two came out of the study, followed by three of Mrs Flittersnoop in different hats of her sister Aggie's, two of Colonel Dedshott, one before he joined the Catapult Cavaliers and one just after.

'Heavens!' cried the Professor. Pushing past them he dashed up the stairs, nearly falling over three more of himself aged eighteen months, cannoned into another Mrs Flittersnoop at fifteen, in fancy dress as Bo-Peep, on the landing. Feverishly he searched the rooms. Everywhere were more and more of himself, at all ages and in all sorts of clothes including one of him

EVERYWHERE WERE MORE OF HIMSELF.

extra specially young with nothing on at all but a big smile.

WITH NOTHING ON AT ALL
BUT A BIG SMILE.

Everywhere there were duplicate Mrs Flittersnoops and spare Colonel Dedshotts and extra copies of various friends and relations. The wonderful liquid had brought every single one of the photographs in the album to life. And they were all saying the same things over and over again.

' Don't take it yet, I've got the sun in my eyes,' and ' Had I better take my hat off first ? ' and ' Hurry up and take it, I must go in and get tea,' and ' I say, what a ripping camera !' and ' Baby want petty sing,' and ' Goo goo.' All of them were saying whatever they were saying when the photograph was taken and couldn't say anything else. But as they were all saying it together it began to get awful. Worst of all, there was half of a policeman who had got taken in one of the photos by mistake, and he kept hopping about on his one leg saying in a half sort of voice ' Pass along p—— ' which was all he could manage of ' Pass along please.'

'Terrible! terrible!' gasped the Professor, guessing what had happened although he hadn't any of his pairs of spectacles on and everyone looked a bit hazy, especially one of Mrs Flittersnoop that had been taken out of focus and was all hazy anyway and kept saying 'Ploof woo woo muffn plith a woogle,' because of course her voice was out of focus too.

'Oh dear,' gasped the Professor, 'supposing I get mixed up with all these come-to-life-photo sort of people and forget which is really me?'

Just then there was a loud bang from the inventory where one of the Professors, age sixteen, had been fiddling about trying to invent something and done an explosion instead.

Out dashed the Professor nearly in time to be hit by a piece of roof. But immediately a rumblety bump followed by loud wowing from inside the house made him dash back. Three of them, age eighteen months, had fallen down the stairs together. A thing he had done himself just after those particular photographs were taken.

'Ploof woo woo muffn plith a woogle,' shouted the out-of-focus hazy Mrs Flittersnoop rushing down the stairs. 'Pass along p—— Pass along p—— Pass along p——' cried the half policeman hopping along from the kitchen where he had been trying to eat half a pie he had found.

Then pr-r-r-ing-g went the door-bell and in came the real Colonel Dedshott.

'Ha! hullo, Branestawm!' he said to one of the photo Professors, age twenty or so. 'Party on and all that, what! Sorry to intrude, you know.'

'Hold it perfectly still while you press the lever,' said the photo Professor, who had been telling someone how to take the photo.

' Ha, ha ! yes, of course,' said the Colonel, not understanding a bit of course but thinking the Professor was talking
some of his professorish stuff which he wouldn't have understood
anyway. ' Been for a holiday ? You're looking well, 'pon
my word you look ten years younger.'

' Hold it perfectly still while you press the lever,' retorted
the photo Professor, who of course looked very much more
than ten years younger than the real Professor.

' Ploof woo woo muffn plith a woogle,' said the hazy Mrs
Flittersnoop, bustling up.

' Goo goo,' said the very young nothing-on-at-all Professor,
trying to climb up the Colonel's trousers.

' How will my uniform come out ? ' said one of the photo
sort of Colonels clanking out of the dining-room.

' What's this ? what's this ! ' roared the real Colonel,
catching sight of him. ' Impostor, scoundrel ! That is not
me at all, I'm me here,' he shouted and chased his photograph
up the stairs. ' Impostor, scoundrel ! ' ' Will my uniform
come out all right ? ' ' Wait till I catch you. Police, police ! '
' Pass along p—— Pass along p——' ' Goo goo,' ' Ploof woo
woo muffn plith a woogle.'

It was more awful than ever. The real Professor dashed
round a corner slap into the real Colonel, and each of them
thought the other wasn't him at all, and while they were
getting explained to each other three of the Mrs Flittersnoops
changed hats, which probably made things no worse.

' Quick,' gasped the Professor after he had told the Colonel
what had happened, so rapidly that the Colonel's head was
nearly as fuzzy as the out-of-focus Mrs Flittersnoop. ' Must
get blotting-paper, dry liquid off photos, then will go back
into album.'

Round the house they dashed, brandishing blotters right and left. The little Professors were caught and blotted up quite easily, but Colonel Dedshott got away from himself three times, and the Mrs Flittersnoop in fancy dress kept dodging the Professor round the banisters.

Slap slap, bump bang, scuffle biff. 'Don't take it yet, I've got the sun in my eyes. Hold it perfectly still . . .' 'How will my uniform come out?' 'Ploof woo woo muffn . . .' Round and round the house, up and down the stairs. The real Professor and Colonel caught each other eight times. The half policeman was hopping about like a canary shouting his half piece half at the top of his voice. Some of the Professors had got hold of blotting-paper and were joining in the chase. Then a window blew open and the draught from the open front door blew them all out of it and down the road, for they were beginning to get a bit light now that the effects of the liquid were wearing off.

'After them!' panted the Colonel, drawing his sword and falling over it.

Out they dashed and down the road. Clouds of Professors and Mrs Flittersnoops were all over the place. A real policeman stopped and gaped at the half policeman, who shouted 'Pass along p——' for the last time and then went zzzzzzzzp back into the photograph he had come from, with the Professor aged twenty.

'Hurray, hurray!' roared the Colonel, throwing his hat in the air and not bothering to catch it, when it landed on the real Professor's head. 'Victory! the enemy is routed.'

And so they were, for the sun had come out and quickly dried the wonderful liquid off the unreasonable crowd of extra sort of people and soon the road was strewn with photographs which the Colonel and the Professor carefully burned, making an awful smoke all over the place, but never mind.

Next day a note came up from Mrs Flittersnoop, written on the back of a picture of an elephant, to say that if the Professor would promise not to do it again she would come back.

'Well, well, well,' he said. 'All the liquid has been used up and I've forgotten the recipe so I shan't be able to do it again, thank goodness. But it was most instructive.'

So back came Mrs Flittersnoop, and the Professor wrote a book about his wonderful liquid but nobody believed it.

THE PROFESSOR
DOES A BROADCAST

-AND THE PROFESSOR AND
MRS FLITTERSNOOP AFTER HIM.

10

The Professor does a Broadcast

'RAT-A-TAT-TAT,' went the knocker on the Professor's door, and an envelope slid plop on to the mat. 'Postman,' said the Professor unnecessarily. He came out of his room to get the letter and ran bump into Mrs Flittersnoop who was coming out of the kitchen to get it too. But Mrs Flittersnoop's sister's doggie, who was staying for the day, got there first, and in about two seconds he was half-way to Pagwell Gardens with the letter in his mouth and the Professor and Mrs Flittersnoop after him.

And goodness knows what might have happened to that possibly very important letter, only at the first bend the dog caught sight of a cat, dropped the letter and went after it. The pussy scratched his nose for him and went up a tree, but meantime the Professor and Mrs Flittersnoop were in a heap in the middle of the road, quite overcome at getting the letter, and four buses, two lorries, and a baker's boy were waiting to go past.

'Well, well, oh dear, dear me,' said the Professor when they got home with the letter at last. 'That was a lucky escape. It only shows you, my dear Mrs Flittersnoop,' he wagged his letter at his housekeeper with one hand and one of his five pairs of glasses with the other, 'it only shows you how the workings of natural instincts in the lower animals, such as the dislike of dogs for cats which you have just witnessed, may at times serve a good purpose for the human race.'

' Yes, Sir, that I'm sure,' said Mrs Flittersnoop, not understanding much but being ever so anxious to know what was in the letter the Professor was holding. The Professor didn't say anything about the natural liking of dogs for letters, but he may have thought a lot about it, being a Professor.

He tore open the envelope and looked at the back of the letter by mistake.

' Tut, tut, practical joke,' he said. ' Blank paper, most annoying after all our trouble. It ought to be stopped.'

He was just going to sit down and write to the Pagwell Police Station to say would they stop practical jokes when Mrs Flittersnoop turned the letter over and read it for him.

' Why, Sir,' she said, ' if it isn't from the B.B.C. and all ! '

' Eh, what ? ' said the Professor. ' Well, if it isn't from the B.B.C. who is it from ? '

' Yes, Sir, that it is to be sure,' she said, and after a bit of talking nonsense at each other because they both thought the other meant something different, the Professor got the letter read properly, though he used the wrong pair of glasses to read it with, which may have made it seem either less or more important than it was.

' Dear, dear, most disturbing,' he said. ' The B.B.C. wish me to do a broadcast from Great Pagwell Broadcasting Station.'

' There now, that will be nice for you,' said Mrs Flittersnoop. ' I only wish I could ask you to do one for me,' and she went out to see about the Professor's dinner only to find her sister's dog had come back all disappointed from the cat and eaten the Professor's chop to make up for his scratched nose. But the Professor had a packet of sandwiches that he'd taken with him the day before when he went out looking for un-expected beetles or something and which he'd forgotten to eat. They were a bit dry, but Mrs Flittersnoop damped them down for him and took them to his study where he was thinking so hard about his Broadcast that he tore them up as if they were post cards, and went round to dinner with Colonel Dedshott of the Catapult Cavaliers.

- LOOKING FOR UNEXPECTED BEETLES OR SOMETHING -

'My dear Branestawm,' said the Colonel, when the Professor told him the news, 'I congratulate you, yes, yes I do. Broadcast, eh? Most excellent. Voice heard all over civilised world and all that. You must rehearse your talk of course.'

'Do what to it?' asked the Professor, who was fishing about in his soup for two pairs of his glasses that had fallen in.

'Rehearse it,' repeated the Colonel. 'You know, read it out a few times to see how it goes. They only let you have so much time to broadcast, I believe. Suppose you hadn't finished and they turned you off for the Children's Hour or something?'

'Dear, dear,' said the Professor, finding his spectacles and putting them on all soupy so that drops of gravy started running down his nose. 'Most alarming. Dear, dear. Children's Hour, did you say? But I know nothing about children. I was going to talk about—er—er—now let me see, what was I going to talk about ? How stupid of me, I must have forgotten.'

As a matter of fact, he hadn't forgotten for once. He'd never even thought of what he was going to broadcast about.

' I think,' went on the Professor, ' I could give an interesting talk on the home habits of the Lesser Littlewort, whatever that is. I know it's something. I must look it up.'

' Do,' said the Colonel, ' and I'll come round and listen to you rehearse.'

*   *   *

A day or so later the Colonel turned up at the Professor's house to hear him rehearse his talk on the Lesser Littlewort. But the Professor had changed his mind three times, forgotten what he was going to do twice, and lost his notes six times. Then he found a page each of four different lots of notes which of course didn't make sense. By the time he had his talk written out the Colonel had had to go home and come back so often that he could hardly remember which house he was at.

' Now,' said the Professor, picking up a sheaf of papers. ' Here is my talk. How long ought it to last ? '

' Oh, about ten minutes, I should think,' said the Colonel, who couldn't stand talks anyway and never listened in for more than nine minutes at a time in case his wireless wore out.

' Very well,' said the Professor, fiddling about with his glasses and getting tangled up with his sheets of paper. ' Wait a minute. Now then, you time me.'

' Right,' said the Colonel, pulling out his watch, which was fast but that didn't matter. ' Ready, go. . . .'

' The Lesser Littlewort,' began the Professor, then his

glasses slipped out of his hand and they had to get sorted out and begin again.

'Go,' said the Colonel again.

'World the in creatures interesting most the of one,' began the Professor and then discovered he was reading backwards from the end. Being used to reading all sorts of queer foreign languages that were written up and down and backwards and sideways as well as in circles and round corners, he hadn't noticed what he was doing.

'Go,' said the Colonel for the third time.

'Ahem,' said the Professor, getting ready.

Just then Mrs Flittersnoop knocked at the door to ask if the Colonel was staying to tea, so they had to have another shot.

'Go,' said the Colonel, fidgeting slightly.

This time the Professor got off beautifully and was half-way through his talk before the Colonel found he'd forgotten to notice the time he started.

'Dear, dear,' said the Professor. 'It is certainly as well I rehearsed. It would have been most awkward if all this had happened at the Broadcast.'

'Go,' said the Colonel once more, wishing he'd never said anything about rehearsing.

Off went the Professor in his best lecture manner. His voice rose and fell. He waved his hands, he struck attitudes, he ticked off points on his fingers, not realising that those sort of things were waste of time, because listening people can't see what broadcasting people are doing.

'There now,' he beamed, finishing at last with his sheets of paper all over the floor and his five pairs of spectacles all over his face. 'How was that?'

'Splendid,' said the Colonel. 'You took half an hour. You'll have to go quicker than that.'

'Oh well, that should not be difficult,' said the Professor. He collected his papers and his glasses and began again before the Colonel had time to say 'Go.'

This time he left out the hand wavings and finger tickings and if his glasses hadn't fallen off half-way through he'd have managed to do it in twenty minutes, but he didn't manage.

'Five minutes longer than before,' said the Colonel, wishing the B.B.C. wouldn't ask Professors to do broadcasts if it meant all this bother.

So the Professor had another go, holding his glasses on with one hand, leaving out all movements and talking ever so quickly. This time he did it in fifteen minutes, but the Colonel said he couldn't understand half what he said.

'Practice makes perfect,' said the Professor, beginning again and getting done in twelve and a half minutes, with the Colonel not understanding anything at all.

'I know what it is,' said the Professor, 'I must open my mouth wider when I talk.'

So he opened his mouth as wide as he could, which was a lot, and talked his talk off so absolutely rapidly with every other word quite distinct that the Colonel's head began to go round and round as it always did when the Professor explained things. And Mrs Flittersnoop, coming in with the tea in the middle of it all, thought the Professor was having a fit and emptied the milk over his head to cool him or something. So by the time explanations had been made and towels had been fetched and more milk obtained and tea had been had, there wasn't time for more than one rehearsal, and that wasn't much good because the Professor skipped four pages by mistake and finished in six minutes.   The milk had gone to his head in more ways than one.

'Well, thank you so much, Dedshott,' he said as the Colonel went.   'I shall manage all right at the Broadcast.   I must open my mouth, hold my glasses and hurry up.   Yes, hurry up.   That will be all right, goodbye and thank you.'

* * *

The next day the Professor put on his best suit, which was the same as the one he wore every day, only with new safety pins in place of the buttons that had fallen off and which he couldn't be bothered to have sewn on again.   Then he went along to the Great Pagwell Broadcasting Station, where they put him in a waiting-room until it was time for him to broadcast.

'Bless me,' he said.   'Dear, dear, I've left my notes at home.'

So of course he had to go home to get them and when someone came to the waiting-room for him he wasn't there.

'The Professor's disappeared,' whispered the someone. He dared not shout because of the broadcastings that were going on all over the place.

'Impossible,' whispered another someone.   'Age of miracles is past.'

'How about wireless?' said the first someone who was rather given to arguments.

'Never mind wireless, find the Professor,' cried an Announcer kind of someone sliding down the banisters because he was too flurried to wait for the lift.   'He's due to broadcast in a few minutes.   The time is now exactly twenty-seven and a half minutes to five.'

He ran back up the stairs because he couldn't slide back

up the banisters, and people went rushing out on foot and on motor bicycles and in vans to find the Professor. It was like a fire station, only worse, because they had no bells to ring and people wouldn't get out of the way.

Seven motor bicycles and three vans drew up in a cloud of dust outside the Professor's house. But the Professor had left, on his way back to the Broadcasting Station with his notes.

Things were getting most urgent. Already the interval was being broadcast, bong, bong, bong, bong. The time is now exactly. . . . The lift went up and down twice as fast as it ought to have done. The gas man called at the Broadcasting Station and got snatched up and rushed into a studio because someone thought he was the Professor.

Then the Professor walked in and was shown the gas meter. Bong, bong, bong. Oh dear, oh dear. The time is now . . .

At last they got things sorted out and the Professor stood in the studio surrounded by grand pianos and arm-chairs while his talk was announced.

' Ten minutes,' he said to himself. ' Mouth wide open. Hold glasses on. Hurry up.'

' Here is Professor Branestawm,' said the Announcer, and went away feeling ever so glad he needn't slide down the banisters any more.

' Ahem,' said the Professor, and opening his mouth wide and holding his glasses on he talked off his talk at a simply terrific rate with his back to the microphone by mistake. But that didn't matter because it sounded better than if he'd faced it because he was talking much too loudly. On he went at a terrific pace. Red lights shone in the studio. Perspiration shone on the Professor's forehead. The microphone made

no sound, which didn't help.   Twice the Professor dropped a
sheet of notes but managed to catch it again just in time.

Three hundred and forty people turned their wirelesses
off thinking he was a foreign station they couldn't get.   Seventy-
two elderly ladies went to sleep thinking he was the interval
signal.   Fourteen rather young children simply howled because they thought he was the Children's Hour and didn't like
him.

ON HE WENT AT A
TERRIFIC PACE·

Several other listening people thought their wirelesses
had gone wrong, and Colonel Dedshott, whose wireless really
had gone wrong and was making the most unreasonable
spluttery squeaky zimming noises, shook his head and said,
' Too quick, too quick, and mouth not open enough.   Can't
understand a word.'

At last the Professor finished. In exactly eleven minutes.
For a moment or so there was silence. Then the Announcer
came in on tiptoe.

' Go on, go on,' he whispered, pulling the Professor under a
piano so that they shouldn't be heard.

' Finished,' whispered the Professor, beaming at him. 'And
only a minute too long.'

' Minute too long,' said the Announcer. ' You've got
exactly seventeen and a quarter minutes still to go.'

' Oh dear !' said the Professor. ' But what can I do ? '

' Do anything, say anything, but say something,' said the
Announcer, pushing him out from under the piano. ' Fill up
time. Explain something. Tell funny story. Anything.' He
crept silently away and the Professor, who couldn't tell a funny
story because he didn't know any, and couldn't explain anything because he knew so many things he couldn't make up
his mind what to explain, did the only thing he could think of
quickly. He started reading his talk all over again, very very
slowly. And all the listeners who hadn't understood what he
was saying before, now understood it, but didn't understand
what it meant because it was so professorish.

But, thank goodness, he hadn't gone very far before the
Children's Hour came on, and as there was a story by Norman
Hunter everything was either all right or else it wasn't.

COLONEL BRANESTAWM
AND PROFESSOR DEDSHOTT

Colonel Branestawm and Professor Dedshott

THERE was going to be a Fancy Dress Ball at West Pagwell and as it was going to be given by the nine and a halfth Squadron of the Catapult Cavaliers, Colonel Dedshott of course had tickets to give away. He gave one to Professor Branestawm, who would have given it to his housekeeper, Mrs Flittersnoop, to pass on to her sister Aggie, who simply loved Fancy Dress affairs and always went as a rather unlikely sort of lady pierrot, because it was the only costume she could make, it not mattering very much what it turned out like, as lady pierrots can look pretty much as they like. They don't always look pretty, but they'd like to.

But Colonel Dedshott wouldn't let the Professor give his ticket away this time. The Fancy Dress Ball was going to be rather special. A general was going to be there. So was the Countess of Pagwell. Prizes were to be given. And the Colonel wanted to take the Professor along and show off a bit about being friends with such a clever sort of person.

'But, my dear Dedshott,' protested the Professor, rattling his five pairs of spectacles about a bit much, 'it is most nice of you to want me to come, but really you know I don't understand fancy dress, I shouldn't know what to go as.'

'Well, if I were you,' began the Colonel; then suddenly he stopped short, for the Professor had clapped his hand to his forehead, sending his five pairs of glasses in all directions.

' Ha ! ' he exclaimed.

' No, no, no,' said the Colonel, afraid that the Professor had thought of an invention that would stop him going after all.

' Yes, yes, yes, yes, yes,' said the Professor, ' I have an idea for fancy dress sort of things for us. Your saying, " If I were you," gave it to me. I will be you, and you shall be me.'

' What say ? ' said the Colonel, beginning to edge away in case the Professor was beginning to go a little queer.

' It's quite simple and most ingenious,' said the Professor, who never minded if he flattered himself a bit because he was slightly used to doing it. ' I will go as you, dressed in an old uniform of yours, and you shall go as me, dressed in some clothes of mine.'

' Ha, ha, ha, lovely ! ' chuckled the Colonel. ' Yes, indeed, that will be most awfully jolly and all that sort of thing what ? '

They had a portion or two of bother over dressing up as each other just at first, partly because the Colonel's second best uniform was the wrong shape and rather too big in parts for the Professor, and partly because the Colonel didn't under-stand the Professor's clothes and got a bit tangled in them. But at last they managed to fix themselves up. The Professor kept his five pairs of spectacles under his Colonel's hat and stuck false whiskers on. The Colonel got the barber to lend him a wig with a high forehead like the Professor's and bought five penny pairs of imitation spectacles to wear on it. Then he stuck some stamp paper over his own whiskers so that they shouldn't show.

' A great success, Dedshott,' said the Colonel, as they

looked at themselves in the glass. 'Upon my word, I believe we look more like each other than each other used to look.'

*   *   *

The General himself came forward to greet them when they arrived at the Fancy Dress Ball, which had taken some arriving at, because instead of being held at the West Pagwell Town Hall as the tickets said, it had had to be held at the North Pagwell Baths, the West Pagwell Town Hall having caught fire in the night.

'Ah, how do you do, Dedshott?' said the General, shaking hands with the Professor.

'Let me introduce my friend Professor Branestawm,' said the Professor, keeping the game up and indicating the Colonel, who shook hands very solemnly with the General. Then they both burst out laughing, and told the General what the joke was. Then he burst out laughing and laughed longer than they did although there were two of them to one of him, because he was bigger.

Then they all went into the hall where everyone was dressed as something they weren't except the Countess of Pagwell, who was dressed simply as a Countess, which isn't simply at all really. And because it was a Fancy Dress Ball, practically everybody thought she wasn't a Countess at all, and were bowing and curtseying and saying 'Your Grace' to the station-master of Pagwell Gardens's cousin,

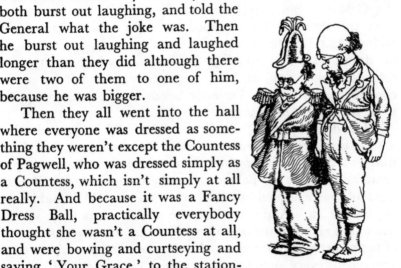

A GREAT SUCCESS

who was dressed as a Chinese Nigger Minstrel or something, and who had said she was the Countess of Pagwell just for a lark, not meaning anyone to believe her.

The Professor and the Colonel had even more of a time of it than they had expected. The Colonel, who liked dancing and did it rather well as long as he was allowed to do it as he liked, couldn't get anyone to dance with him because they thought he was the Professor and guessed that professors wouldn't be able to dance much and might tread on their toes. The Professor, who, of course, couldn't dance at all except a few steps of a Crashbanian war dance which consisted chiefly of running round backwards in circles with your arms folded behind you and one eye shut, found himself carried off to dance with all sorts of charming ladies who rather cared for the Colonel. But they began to think they'd been mistaken after the Professor had stepped on them a bit. And what with that and being swung round and round in time to music he didn't like, and treading on balloons which went most disconcertingly pop at him, and getting all smothered in confetti and things, the Professor began to think he would like to be back in his inventory.

' Oh dear, oh dear, this is awful for me,' he gasped after a tape that held his uniform round him had gone bust four times, so that he disappeared inside the Colonel's too ample tunic and had to go behind somewhere to haul himself out. Then of course he couldn't get used to being a soldier and keeping his hat on. And every time he raised it to a lady, which was about eighteen times a minute because there were so many of them there, only thank goodness quite a lot were dressed as gentlemen, every single time he raised his hat out fell all his pairs of spectacles.

But by this time everyone had found out that the Professor-looking man was the Colonel and the Colonelish one the Professor.

At last the Professor and the Colonel managed to catch hold of each other as they were being swept past one another,

THE PROFESSOR BEGAN TO
THINK HE WOULD LIKE TO BE
BACK IN HIS INVENTORY ·

and they hung on to a very stout and unlikely looking palm tree to talk.

' Oh, let's go away somewhere quiet,' gasped the Professor.

' This being each other sort of idea of yours, Branestawm,' panted the Colonel, ' was all very well for a minute or two, but these Professor sort of clothes of yours are awful to keep on long. I don't know how you manage it.'

' Why you ever joined those Catapult Cavalier kind of

soldiers is more than I can tell,' said the Professor, disappearing inside his tunic again as the tape went bust once more.

'I can't stand it,' he said, all muffled like from inside. 'I know,' he added, suddenly popping out of the too big tunic so suddenly that he made the Colonel jump ; 'let's go into a room and change back.'

'Good idea,' grunted the Colonel. So they went into a room but it was the refreshment room, and some jolly people made them have eight ices and goodness knows how many lemonades before they could get away. They tried another room, but it wasn't a room, it was the way out, and anyway it was locked. They tried three more rooms, one of which was full of not-being-used bathing costumes and ready-to-be-used towels belonging to the North Pagwell Baths, and two of which were the same room with two doors only they didn't know it, and as they each went in at a different door they suddenly came on each other, thought they were someone else, said, 'Oh, ever so sorry, pardon me,' and went out again.

But at last they found a little cupboard sort of room where after a lot of struggling and bumping about they managed to change back into their own things again. But not before they'd tried twice at coming out with a leg each in the same pair of trousers.

'And now, my dear Dedshott,' said the Professor, looking at him through his different pairs of spectacles in turn because it seemed so nice to do it after having had to keep them all hidden away in the Colonel's hat, 'I think it is high time I was getting home to see to those inventions of mine.'

But whether it was high time or low time or middle sort of time, the Professor had no chance to go home, for just at that moment screams went up from among the dancers and pandemonium began to reign.

'My pearls! My pearls! My priceless pearls!' screamed a voice that neither of them recognised as that of the Countess of Pagwell, though that's whose it was.

People rushed about. Doors were slammed. Shouts went up, and there was such a to-do that nobody could hear what anyone was saying, but as none of them wanted to hear, that didn't matter much. But what did matter most frightfully much was that the Countess of Pagwell had gone all collapsed, been carried into the refreshment room, where she drank an entire jug of lemonade and went on shrieking about her pearls.

The General came striding across the floor to the Professor and the Colonel, trod on a piece of once-was refreshment and sat down bump, but immediately recovered himself and went up to the Professor.

'Colonel Dedshott,' he said, thinking of course that the Professor was really the Colonel dressed up in the Professor's clothes because he didn't know they'd changed back. 'Please go out and take command of the guard. Surround the building and let no one go out. The Countess of Pagwell's pearls have been stolen!'

'But I'm Professor Branestawm,' protested the Professor.

'Tut, tut, yes, yes, I know

WITH A LEG EACH IN THE SAME PAIR OF TROUSERS ·

all about that,' said the General, still thinking the Professor was the Colonel and that he was trying to keep up the game of being the Professor. 'But we must forget about that now, this is urgent.'

' But I tell you,' stammered the Professor, ' I really am **me** and he's him,' he pointed to where the Colonel had been, but he wasn't there any longer. ' I don't understand soldiers.'

But the General had lost patience and pushed him out of the door, where a detachment of Catapult Cavaliers stood by their horses. As soon as the Professor appeared they all sprang into their saddles except the Sergeant, who helped the Professor on to another horse much bigger than all the rest, because it was a Colonel's horse.

' I—I—I—here, stop, let go. I—I—I,' began the Professor, but the Sergeant who knew all about the Professor and the Colonel dressing up as each other simply thought the Colonel was being funny and he laughed a bit. Then the Professor fell off the other side of the horse and the Sergeant and all the Cavaliers laughed a great deal.

' Oh dear, but this is awful,' thought the Professor. ' Everyone thinks I'm the Colonel and the more I say I'm not, the more they think I am. Oh, whatever can I do with all these soldier sort of people with their horses and everything.'

Again the Sergeant pushed him on to the horse, and the horse, who didn't understand what the joke was supposed to be about and wasn't used to Colonels falling off the other side of him, began to trot off. The Professor flung his arms round its neck and hung on somehow while the Cavaliers trotted after him.

' Give them orders, Sir,' whispered the Sergeant, cantering up beside the Professor. He'd begun to think perhaps the

Colonel had had too many jellies in the refreshment room, and that was why he had gone so wobbly. ' Give them orders,' he urged again, in a hoarse whisper, possibly because he was a horse sort of soldier.

' Goodness me ! ' thought the Professor, still hanging on, ' I shall have to give some orders of some kind or I'll be getting carted about on this horse for ages.'

So he opened his mouth and shouted, ' 'Shun, slope arms, hard a starboard, at the double, two four six eight ups a daisy, belay there, well played, and don't let anyone out,' saying everything he could remember that he had heard people shout at other people, and some of which he hoped would be Catapult Cavalier sort of orders but none of which were.

' Let's see what they'll do about that,' he thought to himself. And he fell off the horse again.

But he didn't see what they did about it because most of them hadn't heard, as the Professor hadn't shouted loudly enough, not being used to being military.

So the Sergeant got him on to the horse again, and to make sure, he tied him on with a bit of string he happened to have in his pocket.

By this time the Catapult Cavaliers were beginning not to think much of the famous Colonel Dedshott, and instead of nobody being let out of the building, everyone was being let out, in bunches, and they were all trying to find the thief who stole the Countess's pearls. All, that is, except the General, who went to see how the Guard were getting on and got such a shock when he saw what the Professor was doing with them that he burst every button off wherever he had a button, and had to sit down just where he was until someone came near enough for him to shout to them to get safety pins. All except him and the real Colonel Dedshott, whom everybody, of course, thought was Professor Branestawm, and whom the Countess was talking to, nineteen to the dozen, asking him couldn't he invent something to find the thief or look in a glass of water and tell them where he was to be found, or multiply the stars by the moon and take away something or other and know by the result how soon, if at all, she would get her pearls back.

And, of course, the Colonel could only protest that he really was Colonel Dedshott and couldn't do very much even of that, because the Countess didn't give him the chance.

Pandemonium went on reigning. The pearls weren't found. The thief wasn't caught. The people in charge of the refreshments had finished them between them and were either asleep under the table or else felt so ill that they wished they were. The General was still waiting for safety pins on the ground outside. The Catapult Cavaliers had gone home and left Professor Branestawm tied on his horse which was moving slowly over the ground nibbling tasty-looking bits of grass and stuff.

' Oh dear, oh dear, oh dear,' groaned the Professor from up on the horse. ' Oh, why did I come to this fancy dress sort of business. I'd have been much better inventing at home. Professors are absolutely no good at fancy dress. I always thought they weren't and now I know. Well, that's something I've made certain of, so perhaps my time hasn't been entirely wasted, but I—oh, aw, oo—er——'

He said this last bit because the horse had stopped rather suddenly and burst the string that held him on and he came down flop on the ground, right beside the General. The horse

MUCH BETTER INVENTING AT HOME (*The professor's invention for peeling potatoes*)

had stopped to see if the General was a dandelion or something, but finding he wasn't it went away.

' General ! ' cried the Professor.

' Safety pins ! ' exclaimed the General, catching sight of the Professor's coat, which of course was fastened with safety pins because all the buttons had come off, and the Professor never could be bothered to have buttons sewn on.

Hurriedly he told the Professor all about everything, and the Professor managed to convince him that he was himself, while between them they fixed the General up so that he could walk without falling to bits, though he had to keep both hands in his pocket and hunch his shoulders up so that he looked most un-general and dis-military.

' Never mind,' said the Professor, who was so relieved to get off the horse that he was ready to feel happy about anything. ' People will think it's some sort of fancy dress.'

Slowly and somehow they struggled back to the Dance Hall, where something seemed to have happened because pandemonium had stopped reigning, the Countess had gone home and everyone was laughing.

' The Countess's pearls ? ' asked the Professor.   ' Have they found the thief ? '

' No ! ' laughed someone. ' She just remembered she didn't wear them after all, because they didn't seem to go with her dress.'

So that was the end of the Fancy Dress affair, except that in the excitement everyone forgot to give the prizes and didn't know who had won them anyway.

And Professor Branestawm and Colonel Dedshott had the most energetic time explaining to the Colonel's two butlers and to Mrs Flittersnoop that they were now themselves and not each other, as they had been when they set out. But they had both got pulled about so much in the excitement and pandemonium that for a long time Mrs Flittersnoop and the butlers didn't believe them and thought there was a joke on. So they very nearly had to live in each others' houses for the rest of their lives.

'Thank goodness everything is all right again at last,' grunted the Colonel as they said good night. 'It would have been awful if I'd have had to go on pretending to be you and try to invent things. I don't know how you do it, it makes my head go round and round.'

'Yes, rather,' said the Professor. 'And thank ever so much more goodness I needn't be you any more and ride enormous great horses and order soldier sort of people about. How you do that I not only do not know, but I have absolutely no desire to know. It makes me go all of a heap.'

THE PROFESSOR MOVES HOUSE

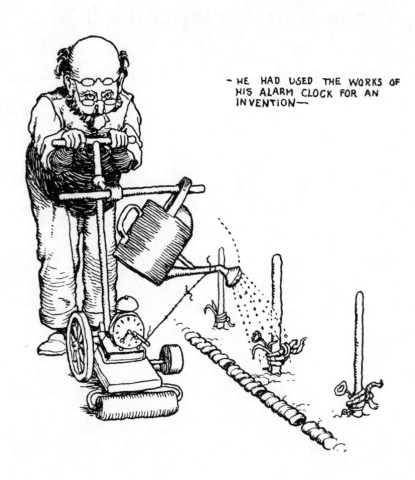

— HE HAD USED THE WORKS OF
HIS ALARM CLOCK FOR AN
INVENTION —

12

The Professor moves House

PROFESSOR BRANESTAWM was sound asleep one morning quite considerably after the time he usually got up, partly because he had used the works of his alarm clock for an invention and partly because he had stayed up unreasonably late the night before trying to invent a way of making seventeen go into three and a quarter, which he rather wanted it to do to make one of his other inventions come right.

And now he was sleeping away and dreaming that his invention really had come right and that he was going along in a nicely cushioned boat on a river of warm cocoa, accompanied by Colonel Dedshott who was rowing with a frying-pan and a cricket bat, and Mrs Flittersnoop dressed in currant pastry of her own making ; while tame fractions cancelled each other out with subtraction signs and well-behaved multiplication sums sang oboe quartettes at them.

But as a matter of fact what was really happening to the Professor was that he was being carried, still in his bed, into a removal van from the Great Pagwell Removal and Warehousing Company. For Professor Branestawm was moving into a new house.

You see, he'd done so much inventing and got the house so cluttered up and stacked about with partly finished inventions and only-just-begun inventions and never-would-get-done-with inventions and might-possibly-one-day-turn-into-something inventions that there was getting to be not room enough for him and his housekeeper to live in peace and comfort. Not that the Professor ever lived in comfort, because he never thought about it, being too much taken up with inventing, which is apt to be an uncomfortable business, especially when the inventions go off unexpectedly in not-meant-to sort of ways, like the Professor's did. And as for Mrs Flittersnoop living in peace—well, she'd learned not to expect to with the Professor about, for she knew that when bangs and sensations weren't happening it was only because the Professor was just busy with something that would cause them to happen before long. Still she always had her sister Aggie to go and stay with.

' Oh, ah, ooooh,' said the Professor, waking up as the moving men, who had been told by Mrs Flittersnoop not to wake him up and who couldn't wait any longer for him to wake himself up, set his bed down bang in the moving van. ' Hullo, what's this ? ' he said, sitting up and looking round in the van. ' Dear me, I don't remember having invented a bed-room like this, but if I did I shall have to uninvent some of it.'

He jumped out of bed, right into the gas cooker, the door of which slammed with a clang on him.

Fortunately the cooker door didn't fasten because it was broken, and the Professor, who had promised to mend it, had forgotten all about it.

' Thank goodness I do forget things,' said the Professor, suddenly remembering he'd forgotten to mend the door and coming out of it just in time to wriggle out of the van about half a second before two wardrobes were pushed in. Then he

DREAMING—THAT HE WAS GOING ALONG
IN A NICELY CUSHIONED BOAT—

MADE HIMSELF SUCH A TROUBLE

went round to see that his inventory was moved properly, and got so absolutely in the way and made himself such a trouble through keeping on popping into the van and bringing out something that had just been put in because he wanted to have a last look at it before it went that the moving men went away to their dinner a bit sooner than they should.

'Come, come, come,' said the Professor when he saw them go, 'this won't get us moved now, will it, the moving men going off to their dinner like this. I think, Mrs Flittersnoop, that you and I had better go on with the moving ourselves till they get back.'

'Yes, Sir, that I'm sure, Sir,' said Mrs Flittersnoop, who as a matter of fact was just going to put on her bonnet and pop down to her sister Aggie's for a bit of dinner herself, but had only got as far as putting on her bonnet and hadn't begun to pop. She didn't at all think the Professor ought to be getting on with the moving because she was quite certain he'd get things muddled. But she knew it wasn't any use trying to stop the Professor getting on with something he'd wanted to get on with. So she took her bonnet off again and gave up all thought of popping down to her sister's, but popped into the kitchen instead and brought out some left-over pieces of meat and things for herself and the Professor to have for dinner while they got on with the moving.

Then they set to work to move things into the vans, and long before the moving men got back from their dinner, which was fairly long, too, because their mummies had told them not to get up too quickly after dinner in case it gave them pains ; well before they got back the Professor and Mrs Flittersnoop had filled up both vans and had no end of things left over with no van to put them in.

' Dear, dear,' said the Professor. ' Most bad kind of management not sending enough moving vans. You'd better pop down to the moving place and tell them we want—let me see,' he reckoned up on his fingers how many more vans would be needed for all the left-over furniture, found he hadn't enough fingers and counted on Mrs Flittersnoop's as well. Then she went and shut her hand in the middle of a most difficult piece of figuring, and the Professor had to give up and make a guess.

' Oh, say we'll need about er—er—oh I suppose, let me see, I should say, er, yes, ten more vans . . . better make it a dozen to be sure.'

So Mrs Flittersnoop, who was only too glad of the chance to pop somewhere even though it was only to the moving place, popped there. Or at least she started to pop there, but she hadn't been popping very far when she popped into the moving men coming back.

Then of course there was a lot of explaining sort of business and waving of hands and scratching of heads and shuffling of feet and saying of this and that. Because the moving men knew very well there weren't a dozen moving vans at the moving place for one thing, and didn't want them if there had been for another. And they were slightly cross about the Professor and Mrs Flittersnoop having

WENT AWAY
TO THEIR DINNER

gone on moving when they weren't there, only they didn't quite know whether they liked to say so or not.

Anyway the end of it was they said they'd get things all right, and Mrs Flittersnoop immediately popped down to her sister Aggie's and had cups of tea on the sofa while she told her she didn't know what the Professor was coming to, really she didn't.

' Moving his own furniture, you know, my dear, and putting himself out, so as you might say. Though when all's said and done maybe it's as well he did, for if he hadn't been doing something like that there's no telling what he might have been inventing. Knowing what he is, my dear, I mean to say, though such a nice well-meaning gentleman, but that absent-minded, though I'm sure I'm that tired I really haven't the strength to tell you a word about it, what with giving a hand with the piano, if you please ; yes and the wardrobes, four of them, and that not counting one the Professor made himself.'

She went on for so long that her sister Aggie, who liked to say quite a bit herself and wasn't getting the chance, began to think of popping down to her Aunt Hetty.

*   *   *

Meanwhile the Professor was having the utmost kind of time with the moving men and everything. First they took out all the things the Professor had put in the vans, then they started all over again packing it in properly. And they got one van nearly done before the Professor discovered he'd forgotten to come out first and he was all packed in too. So that meant another go. But at last everything was ready and off they went, with the Professor sitting on top of the van because he'd happened to be up there admiring the view of

Pagwell Docks through a telescope of his own invention when the van started, and thought he might as well stay there.

- A TELESCOPE OF HIS
OWN INVENTION

At last they reached the new house. At last something was getting done. At last the move would possibly soon be over. The men set to with a will unloading the things. The Professor found the gas and water men hadn't been and there was nothing to boil a kettle on for tea and no water to put in it anyway. So he toddled down to the Pagwell Gas and Water Company and Mrs Flittersnoop arrived while he was gone and began getting tea ready, not knowing about anything as you might say.

'You are my heart's delight,' she sang, so much out of tune that it sounded more like 'The Bluebells of Scotland,' but not very much like them.

She put the kettle under the tap and twiddled the tap on,

but of course nothing happened. She twiddled it off again, and still nothing happened. She tried the other tap and then both taps, and nothing kept on happening whatever she did.

'Oh dear, dear, if that isn't some more of the Professor's doing I'll be bound,' she exclaimed. 'I'd better see if the gas is all right.'

As a matter of fact, if she'd seen just then, she'd have found that the gas, although it might be all right, simply wasn't there, because of course it wasn't connected up any more than the water was. But as she reached out her hand, one of the moving men fell downstairs and got all rolled up in the stair carpet, so she went out to help him get untangled and got tangled up herself.

'What's the use of next day?' the Professor was saying to himself as he came back from the Pagwell Gas and Water Company, who had said they'd send a man next day. 'Gas and water tomorrow won't make tea today, or at least I don't think they will, although of course, if one considers time as a measure of space in the same way as inches and yards one might perhaps work out a theory by means of which, by boiling the water last week and not using it until next Thursday, the tea we ought to have today might have been ready yesterday. I don't know that such a theory is supportable in ordinary practice, but one never knows. Dear me!'

He'd been thinking so hard he'd gone in by the side door and walked down into the cellar by mistake, and found himself face to face with the gas meter and water pipes.

'There now,' he said. 'Talk of gas and water and you find yourself in the cellar. I believe that's a proverb or something.' He had another look at the gas meter and suddenly got an idea.

'Now, now, now,' he said. 'Whatever am I thinking about?' He thought a bit and found he couldn't remember, but anyway it didn't matter. 'Here am I a professor and all and getting worried because the gas and water aren't fixed up. Why, I know what I shall do. I shall just invent a way of fixing them up and everything will be lovely.'

He ran upstairs just in time to miss Mrs Flittersnoop as she ran out to help the man in the stair carpet. Hurriedly he shuffled about amongst nearly everything except what he was looking for until at last he found some of his inventing things. Then down he went again into the cellar and had everything to bits in about half no time. He fixed up a pipe here and a tap there. He turned this nut and that. He got the gas meter all sideways. He did goodness only knows what, but he fixed up the gas and water, which was something.

'There now,' he said, rubbing his hands and making a bit of a clatter over it because he had a hammer in one hand and a spanner in the other that he'd forgotten to put down. 'That seems all right. I'll go up to the bathroom and see if the water's coming through.'

So up he went, stepping over Mrs Flittersnoop on the way without knowing it was her because she was so wrapped up in the stair carpet.

Happily some more moving men coming in with a sideboard noticed the carpet wriggling about, and guessing that carpets aren't supposed to wriggle, they undid it, and Mrs Flittersnoop was able to get back to the kitchen and try the gas.

She struck a match and turned on the gas ring.

Whoosh, out went the match and Mrs Flittersnoop jumped

back in alarm.   For out of the holes in the gas ring shot shower of water.   Like a fountain it was.   Rather pretty if you wanted fountains, but most unsatisfactory if you wanted gas.

'Oh, my goodness me now!' she screamed, and without stopping to think she might as well get the kettle filled while there was water about, she rushed out into the garden to see if the Professor was coming.   She looked up the road and down the road but saw no sign of him.   She looked across the fields and along a side lane, in fact, everywhere she could think of. But she didn't look in the one direction from which the Professor was coming.   She didn't think of it.   You can't blame her for not thinking of it.   The Professor was coming down from up above!   Yes, he was!

With a most terrific bang and showers of all sorts of something he landed right in the middle of a clump of bushes, while pieces of house scattered themselves about in the most untidy way.

Mrs Flittersnoop screamed and rushed back into the kitchen, found the water was still swishing out of the gas ring, screamed again and rushed out followed by all the moving men who were so startled they ran out with the sideboard, forgetting to put it down and wondering why it was so hard to run at all fast.   The postman came with an advertisement sort of circular about vacuum flasks for carrying tea in, but too late to be of help.   The landlord called to see if everything was all right and fainted at once because she was a lady landlord, and therefore not so hardy in the face of upsets as a man landlord might have been.   Colonel Dedshott of the Catapult Cavaliers rode by on a borrowed bicycle and went simply miles past the house because he didn't recognise it, as half of it wasn't where it should have been, it having come out after the Professor when the bang went.

'Oh dear, dear me, how stupid,' said the Professor, coming out of the bushes on the wrong side and nearly falling into the lily pond. 'See what comes of trying to invent without all one's inventing things to hand. This moving business is most upsetting.'

Of course you can guess what the Professor had done. He'd got mixed up with the pipes and things down in the cellar and fixed up the gas to the water pipes and the water to the gas pipes. That was why Mrs Flittersnoop saw such a pretty fountain of water when she turned on the gas ring. And that was, oh dearie dearie goodness gracious why, when the Professor lit a match to see if the water was coming through the bath taps, gas came through instead and everything went bang.

The Professor, of course, couldn't live in the house now, with part of it all to bits and the gas and water all muddled up. So the moving men had to cart everything back to his other house again and when they got there the Professor found the Pagwell Gas and Water Company had sent a man earlier than they had said, but sent him to the wrong house, and the gas and water had been cut off. But fortunately the gas and water man happened to be Mrs Flittersnoop's sister's cousin's young man, and she met him coming away from the house and brought him back to fix the gas and water up properly, and they were able to have tea, though it was supper-time by then.

'And now, I suppose we shall have to start moving all over again, oh dear me, yes I do,' said the Professor, passing a lighted match very gingerly over his tea in case it was made from gas instead of water, which of course it wasn't.

But thank goodness they hadn't to do anything of the kind. The Professor had cleared up and thrown away such a lot of stuff he could do without in getting ready to move first of all that he found the house he had been living in was now quite big enough for everything he had left.

So he stayed where he was. And the Pagwell Gas and Water Company would have made him pay no end of money for making the gas go bang only he'd been rather nice to the chief gas and water man once by helping him get untangled out of an awful mix up of figurish sort of arrangements which the gas and water man didn't understand, but which of course the Professor knew absolutely more than everything about. Then there was the landlady and her busted-about house. She might have been slightly nasty only it so happened that she'd just won a stack of money for a crossword puzzle she hadn't thought she could do.

' Now the next time I move,' said the Professor to himself, ' I shall have a special sort of furniture van that I shall invent, and it will have——'

But just then the telephone rang with Colonel Dedshott at the other end asking what had happened about the move and where was the Professor if anywhere. And by the time the Professor had explained everything to the Colonel five times because the Colonel's head kept going round and round, like it always did when he listened to the Professor explaining things ; by that time it was not only past the Professor's bed-time but also he'd forgotten about the sort of furniture van he was going to invent, so there wasn't any trouble over that anyway.

But that night the Professor dreamed his same dream all

over again that he'd dreamed when the move was starting, with the boat on the river of warm cocoa and the tame fractions and the oboe quartettes. Only this time right in the middle of it the cocoa went off bang and the Professor found he had fallen out of bed.

SHE
ALWAYS
HAD HER
SISTER
AGGIE.

PANCAKE DAY
AT GREAT PAGWELL

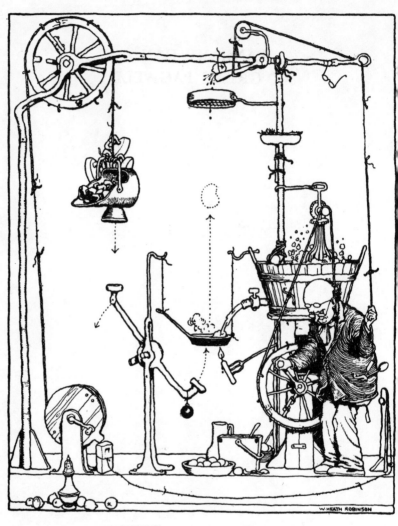

THE PANCAKE MAKING MACHINE·

13

Pancake Day at Great Pagwell

PROFESSOR BRANESTAWM came out of his study with five slightly fat envelopes in one hand and five neatly printed cards in the other.

'Mrs Flittersnoop,' he called. 'Would you mind posting those invitations for me.' He handed her the five cards and took the five envelopes back into his study with him, tore them open, took a pair of his spectacles out of each envelope and put them on just as a tap came at the door.

'Come in,' said the Professor, and Mrs Flittersnoop came in to ask who were the invitations for, because they weren't addressed.

'Dear me,' said the Professor, 'Neither they are.' He looked at the crumpled envelopes out of which he had taken his spectacles. 'Now who can have done that?' he grumbled. 'It's that dog of your sister's again, Mrs Flittersnoop!'

'Begging your pardon, Sir,' said Mrs Flittersnoop, who was so used to the Professor that she saw at once what had happened. 'You must have put your spectacles in the envelopes instead of the cards and given me the cards instead of the envelopes.'

'Well, well,' exclaimed the Professor, 'so I must have, dear me. How strange we professors are, to be sure.'

Then he suddenly looked up and said, 'But really, Mrs

12

Flittersnoop, it is just as well I did give you the cards instead of the envelopes, bless me, or my five friends would be getting a pair of spectacles each, which I doubt if they would under-stand, and they might have thought me odd.'

The Professor carefully put the cards into the envelopes doing his best not to get them mixed, but getting them fearfully mixed all the same, though it didn't matter, because he'd forgotten to write any names on the cards.

At last the invitations were posted and the Professor sat back in his chair, rubbing his hands to think of the great day that was coming, but not rubbing them too hard in case it didn't turn out to be such a great day as he expected.

*   *   *

Colonel Dedshott of the Catapult Cavaliers got his invita-tion just as he had finished his tea.

' Professor Branestawm requests the pleasure of the company of dot dot dot dot dot dot dot,' he read,

(because the Professor hadn't filled in his name, so there was only a row of dots in place of it)

' at his house on Tuesday, February 9th. Tea and Pancakes at 4.30.'

' Ha ! Invitation ! Nice of him,' grunted the Colonel, who didn't feel much like tea or pancakes as he'd just had five cups of tea and nineteen slices of bread and butter, not to mention numerous cakes. ' Was going to Old Catapultonians Reunion, but shall put it off. Dear old Branestawm. Always glad to see him. Don't care for Old Catapultonian Reunions anyway, what ! '

The Mayor of Pagwell got an invitation too, threw it away thinking it was a circular, had it given back to him by the

Assistant Mayor who knew it wasn't because he'd had one as well, and wrote very elaborately to say he would be charmed to give the Professor the pleasure of his company.

Another of the invitations went to the Librarian of the Pagwell Central Library who used it as a bookmark and nearly forgot to go, while the fifth arrived by mistake at the fire station and was sent by the fire engine back to the Professor's house because the firemen knew him. Fortunately, the Professor had met the Vicar of Upper Pagwell for whom the invitation was really intended, in the street, in the meantime, and asked him again, so it was all right. Only Mrs Flittersnoop invited all the firemen because she rather liked one of the dark curly-haired ones, and couldn't very well ask him without all the others, so it was a good job there were only four of them, though it was all too few at a fire even if it was quite enough at a party.

Presently it was Tuesday. Tea was laid. The Professor's spectacles were all mis-laid and four of the visitors were absolutely de-layed because they were the four firemen and there had been a slight fire at the fire station and they'd had to stop to put it out.

' My dear friends,' said the Vicar of Upper Pagwell, standing up and beaming at everyone. ' The esteemed Professor Brane—need I add Stawm?—has asked me to say a few words of welcome to you all. The Professor has invited us here today for a very special purpose. What is that purpose? Is it to drink his tea? Yes, and yet again, no. There is something else, my friends, of greater moment even than that. Can you, I wondah, guess what that something is?' He leaned forward on the table and beamed over his glasses at the guests, some of whom were wondering when the pancakes were coming and some of whom were wondering if there was to be a collection, because the Vicar usually talked all mysteriously like that when he was going to have a rather special collection for something.

The Professor, who had been secretly searching for his spectacles, and had found one pair under the tablecloth, one pair inside the tea-cosy, one pair in his pocket, one pair down his neck, and was still looking for the other pair, suddenly caught sight of the Vicar's glasses, and thinking they were his, he just took them off the Vicar's face and put them on his own. That rather put the Vicar off his little speech and he hummed and er-er-erred a bit, then went on, ' I appeal to you to give generously to this collection which is to provide ironholders for the poor natives of South Crashbania,' and sat down rather more suddenly than he had intended, for the Professor had moved his chair away while he was looking for his spectacles.

There was a little applause at this, though it was probably meant more for the Vicar's kind words than for his sitting on the floor so suddenly, and certainly not at all for the collection. Then Mrs Flittersnoop came in, followed by her sister Aggie's little girl, with the tea and the four firemen who didn't feel quite comfortable, as they hadn't had time to wash properly after the fire, dropped three halfpence each into their cups of tea, thinking it was the collection coming round.

Then the Professor stood up.

' Ladies and Gentlemen,' he said, and Mrs Flittersnoop and her sister Aggie's little girl, who had stayed to see what was going to happen, bobbed little curtsies and nearly spilt the tea they were holding.

' Ladies and Gentlemen,' said the Professor again, ' I have asked you all here today to show you an invention I have

invented.   It is something that has never been done before.   It
will be welcomed throughout the world as the greatest er um
invention since the—er um—since the—er er——'

'Bravo!' cried Colonel Dedshott, beginning to applaud like
anything, but stopping rather suddenly when he found nobody
else was doing it.

'I have—er er——' went on the Professor, 'that is to say,
never before—er um—for the first time in history of ah—um—
er—I will show you my invention and you may judge for your-
selves.'

He stepped across to the folding doors that closed off the
dining-room from what was supposed to be the drawing-room,
but which.was the Professor's study.   He flung open the doors,
one of which caught the Mayor's chair and whisked it away,
letting the Mayor down bump this time, so the Vicar helped
him up.

'Behold!' cried the Professor.   '. . . Oh, er, ah, pardon
me, I must have made a mistake or something.'

There was nothing in the Professor's study except the usual
fearful muddle of nearly everything that was always there, if
you can call that nothing, which of course you can't really,
but you see what it was.   The new invention wasn't there.

'Oh, I remember now,' said the Professor, unfastening the
safety pins that kept his coat together in place of the buttons
he couldn't remember to have sewn on, and looking at a piece
of paper he had taken from his waistcoat pocket.   'I left it in
the kitchen.   Wait a minute, don't go away, I'll go and get it.'

And off he went, while the others looked at each other, and
wondered when the pancakes were coming and tried to think
of chatty things to say, but couldn't think of any except the
Mayor, who wasn't sufficiently recovered from sitting down

bump to say anything, and the Vicar, who had had enough of saying things for the time being and was going to let someone else have a go.

Colonel Dedshott screwed his eyeglass into his eye and dropped it out again seven times, then he was just getting himself ready to say ' Bravo ' again and applaud a bit more to keep things going as it were, when there was a most unmentionable bumping and rattling outside the door, and presently the Professor began to come in very slowly and difficultly because he was all surrounded and tangled up with a sort of machine of some kind.

It was the great invention.

' My guess is that it's a cinematograph,' said .the Vicar, thinking he might as well be a bit jolly.

' I think it's a fire escape,' piped up the dark curly-haired fireman, and Mrs Flittersnoop said ' Bravo ! ' very softly to herself, which made her choke rather because she'd just taken a mouthful of tea.

By this time the Professor had got himself untangled from the machine.

' Behold,' he said, ' my greatest and latest invention, the Pancake-Making Machine.'

' Bravo ! ' roared Colonel Dedshott, and everyone applauded this time, not because they knew why, but because a bit of applause seemed called for somehow or other.

' This is Pancake Day,' went on the Professor, taking his four pairs of spectacles off, and getting them just as mixed up as he usually got his five pairs. ' It is a festival that is inclined to die out, because although people like pancakes they won't bother to cook them. Too much trouble. Too much mess. That is what people say.'

At this Mrs Flittersnoop said ' Bravo ! ' out loud because she was one of the people who had said that to the Professor.

' With this machine,' said the Professor, ' pancakes are as easy as pie to make.'

' Begging your pardon I'm sure,' put in Mrs Flittersnoop, ' but pie isn't easy to make, Sir, that it isn't, not unless you've got a light hand with the paste, not but what my pies aren't always what they should be and no great trouble either, Sir, but you know what folks is—are,' she finished.

' Er—er—yes,' said the Professor. He put some of his pairs of spectacles on and crammed the rest in his pockets where some of them fell through holes on to the floor. He was going to say a lot more about pancakes, but Mrs Flittersnoop had put it out of his head, so he thought he had better demonstrate the machine.

' Here,' he explained, pointing to different parts of the machine, ' are the flour bin, the egg receptacle, the milk churn, and the sugar canister and the lemon squisher.'

' Squeezer,' murmured the Mayor, who didn't agree with funny words, and the curly-haired fireman who was sitting next to him thought he meant squeeze Mrs Flittersnoop, so he tried to, but she was so thin and bony he hurt himself.

' This is the pancake pan,' went on the Professor, getting all worked up and excited, ' and this is the thicknessing regulator, by means of which you can have pancakes any thickness you like.

' Here is the centrifugal tossing gear with adjustable self-changing height regulator, and my own patent device for calculating the number of tosses required for pancakes of different thicknesses.'

' Will it go wrong ? ' asked the Library man, who had heard about the Professor's machines before.

'Certainly not,' said Colonel Dedshott very quickly, because the Professor's explanation was making his head go round as usual. As a matter of fact he knew the Professor's inventions a great deal better than the Library man and thought it definitely likely that this one would go wrong, but he was going to stick up for the Professor. His military training had made him awfully fierce and earnest about sticking up for people.

'Now,' said the Professor, 'for the Pancakes.'

He pulled a lever, turned a handle, twiddled a knob, and pressed a button while everyone looked on hoping the pancakes would be a success, but not caring so very much as long as there were plenty of them because they all felt most unmentionably hungry by now.

Colonel Dedshott almost wished he'd gone to the Old Catapultonians Reunion because there was a dinner to do with it.

'Fiz whirrrr pop chug chug ps-s-s-s-s clang,' went the machine. Wheels went round. Splutterings occurred. There were floppy sounds and hissing noises. Then suddenly there was quite a loud pop and a pancake shot up into the air, turned over exactly once and dropped back into the machine.

'Bravo!' cried the Colonel, beginning to applaud again, but the Professor shushed him.

More fizzes and hisses and whirrings came from the machine. A plate which had been heating over a sort of a gas-ring kind of arrangement but which worked without gas, was slid forward, the pancake dropped daintily upon it, all rolled up and sugared, and wearing the Professor's fifth pair of spectacles which he had dropped into the machine while he was inventing it.

'*Voilà!*' said the Professor, handing it to the Mayor, who

ate it all up, but left the spectacles like a fish bone on the side of his plate, while the eyes of the four firemen goggled so much they nearly fell out on the table.

'Bravo!' cried the Colonel again, rather faintly this time, because he wasn't sure if it was time to applaud yet, and partly because he was so empty inside himself.

The Professor manipulated the machine again, there were more fizzings, another pop, and soon another pancake, which was given to the Assistant Mayor, who ate it even more quickly than the Mayor, because he hadn't had such a big dinner.

'I believe it will go wrong,' said the Library man, who hadn't got a pancake yet.

The next pancake went to the Vicar, and the next should have been for the Library man only the Mayor got it first. Then the four firemen began to clamour slightly because their turn seemed so long coming round and they were used to having everything happen fearfully quickly. You know: 'ding-a-dong, fire, fire, boots on, helmet on, ding-a-dong, rush a rattle, ladders up, hoses out, fire out, ding-a-dong home again.'

The Professor turned the machine on a bit quicker and managed to get pancakes round to almost everyone, while the Mayor was able to stop three that were passed his way round.

'Now it *will* go wrong,' said the Library man.

'Bravo,' said the Colonel with his mouth full, his enthusiasm getting the better of his manners. 'Wonderful, marvellous um yum, delightful, what!'

The four firemen finished their pancakes just five times as quickly as the Mayor took over his first one, which was exactly three and a half seconds less than it took them to get the fire engine out on a fine day, and passed their plates for more.   The Mayor passed five plates, four for himself and one for the Assistant Mayor.

Professor Branestawm turned the machine on full speed. Pancakes came rolling out.   The party was beginning to be most successful.   Then all of a sudden there was a loud click and an extra whizzy whizz from inside the machine and the Professor came over all pale.

'Dear me !' he began, while Mrs Flittersnoop, who was half-way through a pancake, hurriedly hid under the table, expecting the worst, though she didn't know what it might be.

'Whiziziziz POP,' went the machine and a larger and thicker pancake than any shot out of the machine higher than it was supposed to, turned over eight and a half times and dropped on the Professor's head, where it enveloped him like an unreasonable hat ten sizes too big.

'Wuff a g-g-g-g-g m-m-m-m-m pwuff,' spluttered the Professor.

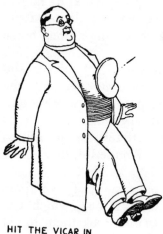

'Whiz, pop,' went the machine and out shot another pancake which made straight for the Mayor, but missed him and stuck to the wall.

'I knew it would go,' began the Library man, leaning back in his chair, but a pancake landed on his mouth, so he said no more. His turn had come at last.

'Whizz pop whizz pop pop pop popetty pop pop,' faster and ever so much faster flew the pancakes.   Thicker and thicker.   Bigger

HIT THE VICAR IN
THE WAISTCOAT

and bigger. They came out flatways and edgeways. They shot high in the air and stuck to the ceiling. One sailed across the room and hit the Vicar in the waistcoat where it may or may not have reminded him of the iron-holders for the South Crashbania natives. Pop, popetty, pop pop pop. It was like a machine gun but much more sploshy.

The Professor struggled out of his pancake just in time

· AND BRANDISHED THEIR AXES ·

for another one to drop over him. Two pancakes were on the clock, four were draped over the light. The Mayor was eating his way through a complete set of pancakes of varying sizes that had fallen in front of him. The four firemen put their helmets on and brandished their axes, but only succeeded in smashing two cups, one saucer, and the sugar basin. Mrs Flittersnoop put her head gingerly out from under the table and was immediately gummed to the carpet by a three-foot pancake two inches thick that had just shot out.

Quicker and quicker fell the pancakes. The pops began to get louder as the pancakes grew bigger. Pop bong bang boom! Roman candles weren't in it. Professor Branestawm was running round the room covered in pancakes and with spectacles sticking out all over him. The Library man got up to go, just managed to dodge an extra huge pancake, sat down exhausted right on the pancake he had dodged, and couldn't move.

'Help!' roared the Colonel. 'The machine's gone wild! Stop it, Professor! By Jove, Sir, the thing's mad. When I was in . . .' A five-foot pancake whistled past the Colonel's ear, shot through the window and suffocated four dozen assorted plants in the garden.

'Wah,' roared the Colonel. His warlike spirit was roused. Bong, bang, boom, thud, echoed the pancake artillery. The Colonel had left his catapult at home. He seized the poker and dashed valiantly at the machine, skewering nine enormous pancakes on his make-do sword as he ran.

- HE SEIZED THE POKER -

Pop, boom, bong, crash, wallop pop whizz bang rattle crash oo—er bong, by Jove crash, thud. How the Colonel attacked the machine ! How the pancakes thudded on the ceiling ! How the poker crashed amongst the cog-wheels ! Everyone got under the table to hide. It fell to pieces under the strain, but a ten-foot pancake flopped rather wearily over all of them so they were hidden just the same.

Crash bang bong smack—'When I was at '—flop crash bing. 'By Jove ! ' Splosh. 'What ! '

At last the fight was over. The pancake machine wheezed and stopped. The poker was nearly tied in a knot, and the Colonel wore on his chest a very small thick pancake which the machine with its last expiring pop had managed to plant there like a sort of medal.

*   *   *

Two days afterwards a most official letter came asking Professor Branestawm to present himself at the Town Hall.

'Dear, dear,' he muttered, 'perhaps the Mayor is going to put me in prison because of the pancakes. Most awkward. I don't understand prisons, I'm afraid.'

But it was all right. The Mayor met him with a smile, though he was half an hour late through having gone to the back entrance of the Town Hall and got himself engaged as a dustman by mistake.

'Meet the Pagwell Council,' said the Mayor. 'Gentlemen, the celebrated Professor Branestawm.'

There was a polite cheer.

'Professor,' said the Mayor. 'Your pancake machine. We wish to purchase it.'

'Yes,' said one of the councillors, ' we want to use cement

in it instead of the stuff pancakes are made of, and use it for laying paving-stones.'

' In that case,' said the Professor, ' I had better invent a way to make it . . .'

' No, no,' said the Mayor, who guessed that once the Professor started re-inventing the machine, it would be something entirely different before he could be stopped. ' We want it as it is.'

So after a bit of bother with the carrier sort of man, who had had no end of bother with the machine because he couldn't get it in his van and had had to tie it on the top from which parts of it fell off rather frequently, the Pagwell Council got the Professor's pancake machine. And they put cement into it. And it shot lovely thick paving-stones out so quickly that the whole of Great, North, South, East, West, Upper, and Lower Pagwell were re-paved in no time, while the Pagwell *Daily Times* had a large article saying how much nicer round paving-stones were than square ones, with a photo of Professor Branestawm printed upside down and his name spelt wrongly underneath.

And the Professor was so pleased that he gave the Vicar enough money to send far more ironholders to the Crashbania natives than they could possibly want.

-EATING HIS WAY THROUGH
A COMPLETE SET OF PANCAKES -

PROFESSOR BRANESTAWM'S HOLIDAY

THE PROFESSOR'S
JELLYFISH CATCHING
EQUIPMENT

14

Professor Branestawm's Holiday

PUFFETY Puff! Zimmety Zim! Tarrumpety clank, zimmety zim! Whoosh! The Great Pagwell Country and Seaside Railway's best express train thundered and rattled and whooshed along, first stop Splashmidoo-on-Sea. And in one corner of a carriage, comfortably on the seat, sat Professor Branestawm's hat, while the Professor had a slight time of it trying to stay up on the rack, having got himself unusually muddled up as usual.

'Er um, funny business this seaside holiday idea,' said the Professor, giving up trying to stay on the rack and nearly getting himself rolled under the seat as the train went rather swishily round a curve. 'I don't know why I came, I'm sure.'

It had been Mrs Flittersnoop's idea for the Professor to go away to the sea for a holiday. 'The change'll do you good, Sir, that I'm sure it will,' she had said. 'And my sister Aggie's cousin Martha who keeps a Boarding-House, she'd be only too glad to have you. Nothing's too much trouble for her, Sir, a real good-hearted one she is and no mistake. And then with a breath of sea air and a walk on the sands, all among the shells and things, Sir, why it'll make another man of you, only do be careful of those jellyfish things if you go in bathing, Sir, not that I hold with much of that kind of thing myself, believing that a good hot bath at home is better than all that salt water that you don't know what it's had thrown in it.'

The jellyfish did it. Professor Branestawm wanted to study jellyfish for a lecture he was going to give at the Pagwell Docks Jellyfish Fanciers' Club, when he could remember to go. So off to Cousin Martha's at Splashmidoo-on-Sea he was going, to be made a different man.

Mrs Flittersnoop and Colonel Dedshott saw him off so that he shouldn't get into the wrong train, and they put him in the non-stop express so that he couldn't get out at the wrong station, both of which he positively would have done if left to himself.

'Well well, rather jolly after all,' said the Professor as he strolled along the sands. Then he put his foot rather unexpectedly on a jellyfish and sat down suddenly.

'Oh oh—er, dear me, most interesting,' he exclaimed, looking at the trodden-on jellyfish through all his five pairs of glasses in turn. 'That must be a new sort of jellyfish. So flat. So squashed out. Um, dear, dear, I must look that one up in my Jellyfish Book.'

So back to Cousin Martha's he went and after some rather botherish business he managed to borrow a sheet of paper out of the laundry book and a pencil with the remains of a point on it, and he wrote to Colonel Dedshott asking him to come down and bring his Jellyfish Book and jellyfish-collecting instruments.

*   *   *

Puffety puff! Zimmety zim, tarrumpety clank, zimmety zim, whoosh! The Great Pagwell Country and Seaside Railway Company's best express train was thundering and rattling and whooshing along, first stop Splashmidoo-on-Sea again.

And on the seat in one corner of a carriage sat Colonel Dedshott with the Professor's Jellyfish Book in his hand, the Professor's jellyfish-collecting tools in his pockets, and his own feet on the seat, which wasn't allowed, but as the train was a non-stop nobody could see.

' H'm, jolly nice, sea, sand, pierrots, what ? ' said the Colonel when he arrived on the front.   ' Will enjoy self when have found Professor—dear dear, confound it, have left his address behind ! '

It was usually the Professor who forgot things, but Colonel Dedshott had had such a time of it finding the Professor's Jellyfish Book, which finally turned out to be under one leg of his bed which was a bit shortish, and looking for the Professor's jellyfish-collecting tools, some of which were in his inventory but most of which were goodness knows where and some of which were in the dustbin, having been thrown away by mistake by Mrs Flittersnoop. The Colonel had got so frantic and flurried trying to get all of them together and not miss the train that he'd left the Professor's letter behind, which had no address on it anyway, and he had forgotten to ask Mrs Flittersnoop where her sister's cousin Martha lived, which wouldn't have helped either, because the Professor had forgotten he was staying there and had engaged himself rooms at five different hotels in succession and was now staying with a motor-boat man who knew some unexpected things about sea serpents.

' Well, well, shall have to walk about till I find him,' said the Colonel coming over all determined.   So off he set, intending to walk both ways along every street in turn till he found the Professor.

He walked both ways along three streets and one way

along one street and found himself on the front again, next door to a pierrot show that was going on.

' Ha, most lucky, Professor giving lecture, what ! ' cried the Colonel dashing forward.

What was really happening was that one of the pierrots was giving an impersonation of a Professor. And somehow or other the pierrot's idea of what a Professor might be supposed to look like was very much the same as Colonel Dedshott's idea of what Professor Branestawm would probably look like while on holiday. And strangely enough the pierrot was giving a comic sort of lecture about jellyfish. So you can see that Colonel Dedshott really had every excuse for the drastic sort of mistake he was going to make.

' Ha ! Branestawm, glad to see you, what ! here is Jellyfish Book and here are jellyfish tools,' he said, going up to the pierrot after the show was over and trying to shake hands with him and give him the book and the jellyfish tools all at once.

' Oh yes, very funny, ha ha, glad you enjoyed it,' laughed the pierrot, thinking the Colonel was having a jolly sort of joke with him.

' What about a cup of something ? ' suggested the Colonel, knowing that the Professor was fond of cups of things except when his spectacles fell in them.

' Oh, thank you very much I'm sure,' said the pierrot man who was also fond of cups of things. So off they went with the pierrot still in his Professor things because he had another show to do soon and didn't want to bother to change.

' Mrs Flittersnoop sends good wishes and all that, you know,' said the Colonel. ' Tell me about those jellyfish things, what ! '

' Who's Mrs Flittersnoop ? ' asked the pierrot, fishing a

pair of spectacles out of his cup which had fallen in because he wasn't used to wearing them.

'Who, what, which!' stuttered the Colonel. He looked at the pierrot. He watched him fish the spectacles out of his cup. He scratched his head, which didn't help because he still had his hat on.

'Sure you feel all right, what?" he asked, beginning to think the Professor must have got sunstroke or something and gone a bit funny. He looked hard at him.

'H'm, does look queer,' he said to himself. 'Pale under the eyes (that was the pierrot's powder). Head looks different shape (that was a dent in the pierrot's wig). Good gracious! Good job I came down and found him.' Then aloud he said:

'Oh, Branestawm, about these jellyfish things. Don't you think you ought to leave them alone for a bit, what, hum?'

'Oh, shut up,' said the pierrot, who thought the jellyfish joke was being taken a bit far. 'I'm fed up with jellyfish. Talk about something else.'

'Fed up with jellyfish!' gasped the Colonel. 'Branestawm,' he said to himself, 'comes down here specially to study jellyfish. Then when I talk to him about them he answers most peculiarly and says he's fed up with . . . tut, tut. Why if he felt all right my head would be going round and round now listening to most complicated descriptions of why jellyfish do this and that.'

'Well, I must be getting back,' said the pierrot, finishing his cup of whatever it was. 'Thanks so much Mr—er er Mr . . .'

'Doesn't remember my name,' groaned the Colonel to himself. 'Only thing he's never forgotten. Must be ill. Sunstroke. Perhaps he gets sunstroke worse than other people because he thinks more. Oo—er. What can do? Must act quickly or may throw himself in sea or something ! '

Hurriedly the Colonel shot out of the shop and round to the Post Office where he spent simply stacks of money on frantic telegrams. One to the Great Pagwell Hospital :

> ' Professor Branestawm suffering from frightful sunstroke. Send doctors and nurses and people. Terribly urgent.'

As soon as he'd sent that one off he thought he'd better send another to be on the safe side in case that one went astray. Then he wrote another to Mrs Flittersnoop, then one to the Pagwell Town Council but couldn't think of what to say, so tore it up. Then he bought himself six shillings' worth of halfpenny stamps, put half a crown in someone else's savings bank, tore a piece of blotting-paper to bits and went out leaving sixpence under the inkpot for the girl behind the counter, who wondered whether she ought to send another telegram herself to the Pagwell Hospital for them to send nurses and doctors for Colonel Dedshott, only she didn't know who he was because he'd forgotten to put his name on the telegrams. Thank goodness Mrs Flittersnoop knew where he was, and yet perhaps it would have been better if she hadn't, for the Professor really was perfectly all right and happily looking for jellyfish two miles along the shore with the help of the motor-boat man, who didn't help much as a matter of fact because sea serpents were more in his line.

* * *

At last two doctors and three nurses arrived hot-foot helter-skelter bing a bing from Pagwell as fast as the Pagwell Motor Ambulance could bring them, which wasn't as fast as it might have been because they lost the way twice and stopped for tea three times.

Colonel Dedshott dragged them hastily down to the pierrot show where the pierrot was just finishing his Professor turn.

' Be over in three quarters of a minute,' panted the Colonel, who had seen the pierrots no end of times to keep watch on what he thought was the Professor.

At last the pierrot finished his turn, other pierrots came

- SEA SERPENTS WERE
MORE IN HIS LINE ·

round for a collection, and everyone went home, except the Colonel, the doctors, and the nurses, who went round and carted the pierrot off to the Ambulance struggling like anything. He bit one of the doctors in the ear, but luckily it was a false ear made of pink rubber and worn over the real one, because doctors knew all about people with sunstroke and rather expected something of the kind. He pulled the other doctor's tie off, which came off rather easily as it wasn't a properly tied-round-the-neck one but only fixed on with a piece of elastic round his stud. He rumpled the nurses' hair, he dug the Colonel in the ribs, he kicked the Motor Ambulance but only hurt his toe. At last they got him packed in, and off they drove with the nurses waving good-bye to Colonel Dedshott

—STRUGGLING LIKE ANYTHING

and the doctors putting their ties and false ears straight, while the Colonel went to have a last look at the sea before catching the next train home.

*   *   *

The next performance of the pierrots was due to start and they couldn't find their funny man who did the comic Professor turn. No wonder they couldn't find him. He was still trying to bite the imitation rubber ears off the doctor in the Ambulance on the way to Great Pagwell.

'Must find him quickly!' said the chief pierrot. 'You go and search for him,' he said to the two pierrots who usually went round with the collection. 'I will keep on singing lovely songs to keep audience happy till you get back.'

So off went the two pierrots and on went the chief pierrot, and before he had sung more than one and a half songs the other two found Professor Branestawm digging up an extra large jellyfish while the motor-boat man was asleep round the corner dreaming about a sea serpent with knots in it.

'He's got a touch of the sun, that's what he's got,' said the pierrots to each other, thinking Professor Branestawm was their funny man still in his Professor things. 'That jelly-fish talk of his has gone to his head. Better hurry him back.'

So getting one each side of the Professor they hurried him along to the pierrot show.

'But dear me, good gracious, let me go at once,' protested the Professor, kicking up the sand in all directions. 'I am collecting specimens for a most important lecture on the lives and habits of eighty-seven kinds of jellyfish.'

'Yes yes, we know,' said the pierrots, thinking they had better be nice with him in case he got rough. 'Everyone is waiting to hear your lecture now. Come on.'

'Well, really this is a most extraordinary way to invite anyone to give a lecture,' spluttered the Professor. 'I certainly will give a lecture on jellyfish if you wish me to. It is a subject I have studied with great interest. But dear dear, wait one moment, there go two of my pairs of spectacles.'

At last, after no end of struggling about and protesting sort of talk from the Professor, the pierrots got him on to their little stage and the audience cheered like anything because they thought he was the pierrot funny man and they liked him.

The Professor didn't understand pierrots and he thought everyone wanted to hear a lecture on jellyfish. So off he started most seriously, and whether it was because the audience were expecting lots of fun or whether it was because the Professor had got his thoughts rather muddled through being hustled so shusshily along the sand by the pierrots, the Professor's lecture on jellyfish was ever so much funnier than the real funny man's funny lecture had ever been. People rolled about in their chairs with laughter. They rolled off their chairs with laughter, but had to pay their twopence for them just the same. Four stout gentlemen in the front row burst two buttons each off their waistcoats. Several people up on the promenade, who had been watching the show free, fell over the rail and had to pay for the chairs they fell into. Shrieks and screams and yells and roars of laughter rolled up from the pierrot show. People left the ice-cream shops and penny-in-the-slot machines and donkey rides to see what the fun was. Even the pierrots themselves were laughing. The Professor couldn't understand it at all.

He was just getting to the end of his lecture and half the audience were all of a heap with laughing and dared not look at him or listen to him any more in case they came to bits, when up dashed the real pierrot funny man with his Professor's disguise a bit out of place. He had managed to bite the real ear of the doctor who wasn't wearing false ones, and escaped in the confusion.

' Impostor ! How dare you ! Hold him ! ' he yelled, rushing up on to the stage.

Twenty-seven deck chairs collapsed flat with a noise like

brisk thunder as the people in them nearly went bang with laughter. The four fat gentlemen in the front row burst their waistcoats off entirely.

For of course everyone thought the second professor coming in like that was part of the show, and anyway they were too limp and flopped out with laughing to care what it was.

'Hold him, hold him!' panted the pierrot professor. 'People tried to kidnap me, but I escaped. He must have planned it so that he could steal my turn.'

'I—er, but that is,' began the Professor. But before he could say anything properly the pierrots shussled him off with

"IMPOSTOR!—" HE YELLED

a bunch of them all round him and carted him along to the police station, leaving their audience lying about the beach in handfuls where most of them had to stay for ages until they felt strong enough to walk home after all the laughing.

'He's an impostor,' cried the pierrots as they surged into

the police station with the Professor all tangled up among
them. 'Pretending he was our funny man and had our real
funny man kidnapped.'

'No, no, no! most wrong, nothing of the kind!' gasped the
Professor.

'Now then, what's all this?' said the police sergeant, taking
out his notebook but finding it all full up with funny drawings
his little boy had made.

At last things got a bit sorted out, and the Professor was
taken into the court before the Magistrate.

'What have you to say for yourself? Good gracious, my
dear Professor Branestawm!' exclaimed the Magistrate. 'Why,
whatever can be the meaning of this?'

'Inky!' shouted the Professor. He dashed across to the
Magistrate, and they shook hands for four and a half minutes
till the Professor's spectacles began falling off into the inkpot.

The Magistrate was an Old Pagwellian! He and the
Professor used to go to Great Pagwell College together, and
the Magistrate was called 'Inky' because he couldn't help
getting ink on his face. He couldn't help it even now, for
the Professor's glasses falling in the inkpot had splashed
him.

'Professor Branestawm is no impostor,' said the Magistrate
sternly. 'It is your man who is the impostor, passing himself
off as Professor Branestawm.'

'No, no, no,' squealed the pierrot. 'I do that for a funny
turn. I found a photograph of a professor in an old newspaper
and copied it for our pierrot show. Look.' He handed up
a most second-hand-looking piece of newspaper. It was a
copy of the Pagwell *Daily Times* with a not-too-good photo of
the Professor printed upside down and his name spelt wrongly,